THE ADVENTUROUS FOUR

TRAPPED!

THE ADVENTUROUS FOUR

TRAPPED!

by
ENID BLYTON

Illustrated by Gavin Rowe

AWARD PUBLICATIONS LIMITED

For further information on Enid Blyton please visit *www.blyton.com*

ISBN 978-1-84135-736-2

First published 1952 by Newnes as *Off with the Adventurous Four*
First published by Award Publications Limited 2003
This edition first published 2009

Published by Award Publications Limited,
The Old Riding School, The Welbeck Estate,
Worksop, Nottinghamshire, S80 3LR

10 2

Printed in the United Kingdom

CONTENTS

CHAPTER ONE

WHICH ISLAND SHALL WE CHOOSE?

A fisher boy stood by his red-sailed fishing boat. He screwed up his eyes in the sun, and watched a little house not far off. Would those three children never come?

He sat down on the edge of his fine little fishing boat. It was called *Andy*, and that was the boy's name, too. Andy was tall and brown-haired and his eyes shone like the blue sea behind him. He drummed his heels impatiently on the side of the boat.

Then he heard a yell and saw three children racing out of the little house he had been watching. "Here they are at last!" he exclaimed and stood up, waving.

Tom came first, a wiry boy of twelve with flaming red hair. Then came the twins, his sisters Pippa and Zoe, their long golden plaits flying behind them. They flung themselves on Andy, almost knocking him over.

"Now, now," he said, fending them off. "You're late. I almost set off without you."

"Sorry, Andy, but Mummy made us finish some jobs," said Pippa. "Anyway, we've got all day, haven't we? And it doesn't even matter what time we get back tonight because Mummy's going to spend the night with a friend. She's asked old Jeanie to stay at home while she's away. And Jeanie's a jolly good sort! She knows we can take care of ourselves, and she doesn't worry if we're with you. If we let her know what we're doing, and who we're with, we can creep in any time we like. So hurray for a day on the sea!"

"Have we got plenty of food, Andy?" asked Tom anxiously. "And some of those sausages?"

"Aye, there's a tin for you," said Andy, grinning. "What a one you are for sausages, Tom! Look down in the cabin and see if you think there's enough food there!"

Tom squinted down into the tiny cabin. Yes, there seemed plenty to eat and drink. Good!

"Help me up with the sail," called Andy. "There's a strong breeze this morning.

We'll scud along at a fine pace."

Once on the sea, the two boys put up the sail. Andy took the tiller. The wind filled the little red sail and the boat sped along like a live thing.

"This is what I like," said Pippa contentedly, letting her hand drag in the cool, clear water. "The look of the sea, the smell of the sea, and the feel of the sea. Lovely!"

"I think every single boy and girl ought to have a boat," announced Zoe. "A boat to row and to sail. There's nothing like it!"

The boat cut into a sudden wave and a shower of salty spray splashed over the twins. They shook their golden heads.

"Lovely!" said Zoe. "Do it again, Andy!"

"Where are we going?" asked Tom. "Have you made up your mind yet, Andy? You said you'd take us to one of the little islands round about."

"I've not made up my mind," said Andy, his brown hand on the tiller. "I thought maybe we'd just cruise round a few, and you could pick one you fancied. We could have a picnic there."

"One with birds, please," said Pippa.

"Yes, with tame birds," said Zoe, "tame enough to let us go right up to them!"

Andy laughed. "Right! Pick one with tame birds then. But don't blame me if you get pecked."

The boat sped on over the water. The sea was a cornflower blue in the distance, but round the boat it was a lovely emerald green, and it glittered as they cut through it.

"The land is getting further and further away," said Pippa. "It's almost as if the coast was going away from us, not us away from the coast! What a good thing there's a stiff breeze."

"Yes. We'd be cooked if there wasn't," said Tom. "Andy, did you catch a lot of fish this week? Was your father pleased?"

"He was fine and pleased," said Andy. "If he hadn't been I'd not have been given this day off. Like to take a turn at the tiller, Tom? She's going beautifully this morning – seems as if she's enjoying the trip as much as we are!"

Pippa patted the little boat. "Of course she's enjoying it," she said. "That's what's so nice about a boat. She comes alive on the sea, and enjoys everything, too. I'd like to be a boat and rush along like this, bouncing and bobbing over the waves."

"Yes, and it must be nice at night to make your bed on the water and hear the little plash-plash-plash against your sides," said Zoe. "And lovely to feel your sail billow out and pull you along!"

The land was now so far away that it was impossible to see even the high church tower. The coast lay like a blue, undulating line on the horizon. The *Andy* had certainly gone at top speed with the wind!

"Let's look out for the islands now," said Andy. "We'll be seeing them soon."

"I suppose we'll be the only people on any of them," said Tom. "That'll be good. I don't like crowds, I'd rather be with a few people I like and go adventuring. That's the life for me!"

"Well, you seem to enjoy people at school all right," said Pippa lazily. "Whenever we come down for your Sports Day you're always right in the very middle of a yelling, pushing crowd of boys – I never see you huddled away in a corner with just one or two."

"Oh, well, school's different," said Tom.

"It's nice being in a crowd then. Ah! I see the first island!"

Everyone looked at where Tom was pointing. It was so small and so far away that at first the girls couldn't see it, though Andy's sharp, long-sighted eyes had actually seen it even before Tom's.

"Yes, that's an island," said Pippa. "What sort is it, Andy?"

"No good to us," said Andy. "Just a half-mile or so of bare rock. Even the birds don't like it much. The waves sweep it from end to end in a storm."

"Wow! It'd be great to be on it in a storm and feel the waves sweeping round my feet," said Tom.

"They'd sweep round your neck!" said Andy drily. "Look, we're coming near it now. It's not much of an island."

The *Andy* swooped nearer. "No," said Tom, "it's a poor sort of island – all seaweedy. I can't see even a bird. We'll pass this one by! On, Andy, on!"

They left the rocky little island behind, and another one loomed up, with yet another to the right.

"This is fun," said Pippa, standing up

and taking hold of the mast. "Andy, do you
know every one of these little islands
scattered on the sea here?"

"Oh no," said Andy. "There are too
many – about fifty or sixty, I should think.
All too small or too bleak to live on, besides

being too far from the mainland for comfort. I know some of them because of the fishing. There are plenty of lobsters and crabs around here. And I've landed on a good few for fun. Now, you watch carefully as we cruise by and see if there's one to your liking – tame birds and all!"

They sailed by island after island. Some were flattish, some had towering rocks, some were bare and some were covered with wiry grass and pink sea-thrift. Most of them were very small and some were joined to each other by long ridges of rock.

"There's one with birds!" cried Pippa, pointing. "Look! And it seems a nice kind of island, with plenty of grass and cushions of thrift. Sail round it, Andy."

Andy took the tiller from Tom and the boat made a tour round the little island. At one part Andy thought it wasn't possible, because a ridge of rock ran right out to the next island. But his sharp eyes caught sight of a little channel where the rocky ridge appeared to break or dip down. Cautiously he sailed the *Andy* slowly along and peered down into the water. It was deep and clear, so on he steered through the narrow little channel between the rocky ridges.

"Well, I think this is the island for us," said Tom. "It looks well-grown with grass, and there are plenty of birds about – especially on that high cliff on the west side of the island. Let's land here, Andy."

Andy looked about for a place to take the boat into. He saw exactly what he wanted – a sloping sandy cove where waves ran up and back. He waited for a big one and then rode in on it. As the wave ran back he leaped out and held the boat, flinging the rope round a convenient rock.

The other children all sprang out on to the wet sand, which felt cool to their hot feet. They began to pull the boat up a little way, but she was too heavy to pull far.

"Now, shall we explore first, or watch the birds, or have a meal?" said Pippa.

"I bet I know what Tom will say," said Zoe, laughing. "He'll want to eat his sausages!"

"That means we'll have to make a fire to cook them on," groaned Pippa. "Let's make him find the firewood!"

"No," said Tom unexpectedly. "It's too hot for sausages. Let's open a tin of ham

15

and have it with the fresh bread Jeanie gave us. We can take plenty of food from the boat and carry it with us until we find a good place to eat it in."

They all chose the food they wanted – a tin of ham, the bread, two crisp lettuces, a bag of ripe tomatoes, and a basket of glossy plums.

"That's what I call a jolly nice meal," said Tom, pleased. "Now, what about drink? I could drink a bathful of lemonade."

"Well, find the bath first," said Pippa. "I've got a bottle of orangeade and a bottle of water here. Perhaps I'd better bring *two* bottles of water – if you're all as thirsty as I am we'll need them!"

They set off, carrying the food. Tom suddenly stopped. "Blow!" he said. "We've left the tin-opener behind as usual. Why do we always forget it?"

"We haven't!" said Andy. "I've got it. Come on! What about having our picnic on top of that cliff? There are plenty of birds on the rocky ledges to watch. We'll get a fine breeze there, too."

"And a wonderful view!" said Pippa.

"*And* cushions of pink thrift to sit on,"

said Zoe. "It's so nice of it to grow in tufts like this. I love the little pink flowers. I say, isn't the sea blue!"

It certainly was – and when they were all sitting on the cushions of thrift, high up on the cliff, it seemed unbelievably blue. The breeze blew strongly and kept them nice and cool.

"This is great," said Tom, opening the tin of ham. "Nobody near us for miles and miles and miles. No trippers. No horrible litter. Just us and the birds and the sea."

"And the lobsters and crabs," said Zoe, pointing out to sea. "There are pots down there, aren't there, Andy?"

"Aye, those flags you can see show where a fisherman has laid his pots. There'll be a line of them on the seabed. One beneath each of the flags. But I don't suppose anyone will be out to check the pots today. They'd have been here by now, if they were coming."

"A very, very peaceful day," said Pippa. But she spoke too soon. It wasn't going to be quite such a peaceful day as she thought!

CHAPTER TWO

HADN'T WE BETTER LOOK OUT?

The picnic lasted a long time. Tom said it was a pity to leave any of the ham, so they didn't. The tomatoes were so nice and juicy that they all ate several each, and Tom got cross because Zoe ate the last one.

"Well, you can have some more – there are some on the boat," said Pippa. "But you'll have to go and get them. No one else wants any."

Tom was too lazy and too comfortable to get up and go back to the boat, so he delved into the basket of plums instead and much enjoyed those.

"There ought to be quite a nice lot of plum trees springing up on this island next year," he said, spitting out his sixth stone. "People coming here will be amazed. I say, look at that gull! It's coming right up to us. Well, you wanted tame birds, Pippa. Here's one for you."

The gull was a young one. It was quite unafraid, and had probably never even seen a human being before. It was very inquisitive indeed. The children watched it wonderingly.

It walked right up to Tom, put its head on one side and stared at him solemnly. Tom put his head on one side too and stared back. The twins laughed.

The gull then stared at Tom's bare feet, lunged at his big toe and gave it an enormous peck. Tom gave a tremendous yell and rolled away quickly. He sat up and rubbed his bruised toe, glaring at the surprised gull.

"What did you do that for? Don't you know a toe when you see one? You're too tame for my liking. Go away and be wild!"

The gull listened, and then walked over to Andy, who held out a bit of bread to it. It pecked at it, swallowed greedily and looked round for more. It walked right over Andy's legs and made for Tom again.

The twins roared. Andy made a noise like a gull calling, and the bird looked even more surprised. It opened its great wings and flapped them, giving an answering call.

"My word, what a wind!" said Tom. "Hey, gull, you almost blew my hair off then. Can't you go and flap yourself a bit further off? Oh, my, he's coming for me again."

The gull caused them a great deal of amusement. It was so very friendly and so very inquisitive. It pecked at the ribbons on the girls' plaits, it stood on Pippa's foot, it even tried to sit on Tom's head but he wouldn't let it. It pecked a plum out of the basket and swallowed it whole, stone and all.

"Here! That's enough!" said Tom, snatching the basket up in a hurry. "You've had the plum I'd got my eye on. Don't you know they're bad for gulls?"

"My word – here come a few of his friends," said Andy, amused. Sure enough three or four more gulls were walking up to join their friend.

Tom stood up. "I feel it's time to go," he said. "I shan't have a toe left to stand on soon!"

But the gulls were scared when he suddenly stood up and with a great sweep of wings they flew back to their rocky ledge on the cliff, where they sat together, looking out to sea. Tom stood watching them and then another bird caught his attention. It was a pigeon, not a gull. A pigeon far away from the land, but flying straight and true towards the island. Tom pointed it out to the others who shaded their eyes and watched the bird until it disappeared from sight behind a rocky hill.

"How strange to see a pigeon all the way out here," said Pippa.

"If that gull's anything to go by, it won't find much to eat," said Tom, sitting down again and rubbing his toe. "Greedy thing!"

By now there was nothing left of the picnic, and all the orangeade had been drunk. Pippa was dozing by the remains, and Tom was settling himself down to do the same.

"Have to take the bags and tin and bottles back to the boat in a minute," said Pippa sleepily. "Who's going to?"

"Oh, let's sit here in peace for a while," said Zoe. "I could do with a nap. But first I'm going to climb up to the top of that little rocky hill and count how many islands there are. I should be able to see all round the island from there."

She got up and climbed the rocky hill, leaving Pippa and the boys dozing in the sun. The hill went up almost to a point, and Zoe sat right at the very top, enjoying the strong breeze and view.

Islands to the left, islands to the right, islands all round! How exciting they looked! How strange that nobody lived on them. They were empty except for the birds. Not even a rabbit lived on the little rocky islands. Zoe gazed at the next island to theirs, the one nearest the marker flags bobbing on the sea and fluttering in the breeze. The two islands were almost joined by the ridge of rock through which was the channel where their boat had sailed. It looked an island much like theirs, but was far rougher and hillier with patches of bracken dotted with boulders running up the hills.

And then Zoe stared. She could see something but what was it? Something white was flying and fluttering in the air. Not smoke. It didn't look like smoke. It looked almost like tiny white birds. She called down to Pippa:

"Pippa – have you got the binoculars? Bring them here, will you? There's something strange on the next island."

Groaning to herself, Pippa climbed the hill and handed Zoe the binoculars. Zoe put them to her eyes and stared through them. Now she would be able to see what the white things were.

"How very odd!" she said. "They look exactly like bits of paper – letters or something! They can't be, though. No trippers ever come to these islands, I'm sure. You look through the binoculars, Pippa, and see what you think!"

Pippa focused the binoculars on the white things. She nodded. "Yes, it's paper of some kind, flying in the breeze. How peculiar. Who would come here with paper and let it loose on an island? It's just nonsense."

By now the boys were interested, too, and they joined the girls at the top of the rocky hill. Each in turn looked through the binoculars, and all of them agreed that for some reason or other papers *were* flying about on the next island.

"But whose papers? And how did they

get there, and why?" said Tom, puzzled.

"Dropped by an aeroplane?" suggested Pippa.

"What! Dropped on a lonely island like that? What for?" said Tom, scornfully. "Or do you mean by accident?"

"Well, I suppose it might have been an accident," said Pippa.

"These islands are off the route of any aeroplane," said Andy. "You'll not see one here from one year's end to another. Those papers could only have been brought by boat."

"I suppose we must just put them down to trippers," said Zoe. "How disgusting! Why bring a load of newspapers – or whatever they are – and leave them there to fly about?"

"It is a bit peculiar," agreed Andy. "But come on now, we can't stay here all day looking at papers flying about. Let's take our own litter back to the boat. And then what shall we do? Explore this island? Make friends with any more gulls?"

"Oh, not that," said Tom hastily. "I can hardly walk as it is, my big toe is so bruised. No, let's do a spot of exploring."

"I'd like to go and see what those papers are," said Pippa unexpectedly.

"Well, that's not a bad idea," said Tom.

"Not a bad idea at all. The thing is, how do we get there? By boat? It would be a bit of a bother to get the *Andy* and sail off again."

"Couldn't we walk along that ridge of rocks and swim across the little channel we went through, and then climb up the opposite ridge of rocks and walk to the next island that way?" asked Pippa.

"Oh, yes! We meant to have a swim, anyway!" said Zoe, pleased. "Let's go back to the boat with our bottles and things, change into our swimsuits, and go off to the next island for the afternoon. We can easily swim across that little channel. It will make it exciting."

Everyone thought this a very good idea. They went back to the *Andy* with their bags of rubbish, and changed into bathing things.

"Lovely!" said Pippa. "This is much better. It's far too hot to wear clothes today. I wonder we didn't come out in swimsuits in the first place!"

The tide was in a little, but the *Andy* was quite safe. The children stowed away their clothes and litter, and put the bottles and the basket into the cabin. Tom got some bars of chocolate and put them into a waterproof bag round his neck.

"Just in case we get hungry before we get back," he explained. "You never know!"

"Well, after that enormous meal I don't feel as if I shall be hungry for about two days," said Pippa. "I shan't want any of your chocolate!"

They set off, and soon came to where the rocky ridge stretched out from their own island. They walked lightly along it in their bare feet. They found that it was better to walk on the lower part, which was occasionally washed by the waves, than on the upper part, which was burned hot by the sun and scorched their feet.

It was fairly easy to cross the ridge, though sometimes they had to clamber round on hands and knees in case they slipped. When they came to where the rocks dipped right down into the sea, making the little channel, they climbed down to where the ridge reached the water.

"Can't see any bottom at all," said Tom, peering down into the channel. "Looks as if the rocks break off. Well, in we go, and swim across. It looks gorgeous!"

They dived in one after another and swam swiftly across the gleaming channel, enjoying the cool water on their bodies. They didn't want to climb out when they got to the other side, it was so lovely in the water.

They swam about for a bit, splashing one another, and clutching at legs, and swimming under the water with their eyes open, watching for anything exciting down below. But there was nothing to see, not even a fish, and at last they pulled themselves up on the rocks opposite.

"Well, I'm still hot!" said Pippa. "Wasn't that lovely?"

"Glorious," said Zoe. "I'm not hot, though. I'd like to climb up the ridge and go on to the next island."

"Well, come on, then," said Andy. "I'd like to go, too."

They clambered along that ridge and came to the next island. It was not as green as theirs, though cushions of sea-pinks grew here and there, and tufts of wiry grass sprang up where there was any earth.

"Now, where was it that we saw that paper flying?" said Pippa, stopping. "Oh, look – that's a bit, I'm sure. Yes, it is – look, blowing over there."

They ran to the piece of paper, which was flapping along like a live thing. Tom pounced on it and picked it up. The others crowded round him.

"It's a kind of document," said Tom. "It's got all kinds of weird numbers and things on it – and look, where it's torn, there's a bit of a plan or something. What can it be?"

"I don't know," said Pippa. "But it looks sort of important to me. Let's go and pick up some of the other papers. They must be somewhere about. This is really very peculiar. Tom, you don't suppose there's anyone here, do you? Hadn't we better look out?"

CHAPTER THREE

SOMETHING VERY PECULIAR!

For the first time the four children felt that there might be someone else on the islands besides themselves! It wasn't really a very nice thought. Where could their boat be? There was no sign of one, although it might, of course, be hidden away in some cove.

On the other hand, someone might have come and gone, leaving behind a mass of papers to blow about. But how very strange, if so!

"Let's find some more papers," said Pippa, and they went forward, keeping a look-out. It wasn't long before they came on four or five more, flapping about in the breeze. They were much the same as the first one they had picked up, except that one was on blue paper instead of cream.

"More figures, more plans," said Tom, looking at them. "It's such tiny writing I can hardly read it. And I wouldn't understand it even if I could read it! Andy, what are these papers?"

"I don't know much about these things," said the fisher boy, slowly. "But it seems to me that they're plans of some kind. I don't know what of. But why they're blowing about here beats me! If they're stolen – and I think they may be – why scatter them over an island? Why not use them, copy them perhaps – and then burn them? Or at least keep them in some safe place? It's very strange."

"Who do they belong to, anyway?" said Pippa, looking all round as if she expected the owner to appear. "Someone must have brought them here. Where's he gone?"

"Goodness knows," said Andy. "But I tell you what I think – I think we should collect all we see and take them back to the *Andy* with us. If they're important it would be the right thing to do, and if they're not – well, it won't matter."

"Yes, that's a good idea," said Pippa, and she picked up a few more. She straightened them out, folded them neatly, and put them together. The others began to do the same.

Then Tom gave an exclamation. "I say! Come and look here!" he cried.

He was behind a rock. The others ran across and saw him bending over what looked like a suitcase. It was open, and from it came the papers that were flying about everywhere! Even as they looked, the wind tugged at another in the case, and sent it high into the air. Zoe caught it. It was a blue one, and had another lot of figures and diagrams on it.

"A suitcase full of papers!" said Andy, amazed. "So that's where they're coming

from. But who put it there? And why has it been left open?"

"More and more mysterious," said Pippa. She looked carefully at the suitcase, which was not a very good one – it was made of imitation leather and had cheap locks. Suddenly she saw that one end of it was badly dented.

"Look," she said. "See this dent? It's had a fall – been dropped from a great height, I should think. Goodness, do you suppose an aeroplane has dropped it?"

"No! It would have been bashed to pieces," said Tom. He looked at the dented end of the case, and then glanced upwards. They were in a rocky spot, open to the wind and sun except behind them where a tall cliff rose up, towering high.

"I bet it's fallen from somewhere on this rocky wall," said Tom. "If it had, whichever end it fell on would be dented by the rock it hit, then the case would burst open its clasps and the papers would fly out one by one in the wind. That's what happened, I think."

"Yes, you're probably right," said Andy soberly. "But it doesn't solve the question of who owns the case, how it got here, and why it fell off the cliff. I rather think there must be people on this island."

"I hope not," said Pippa. "I don't feel as if I should like them very much."

They looked up at the bracken-covered cliff above them. About two-thirds of the way up they spotted a dark area. Was it a cave of some sort?

"I'll go and see," said Andy, and swiftly began to clamber up. The others watched him in silence. Andy came to the dark place and looked into it – it *was* a cave! He turned round and made a sign to the others to be silent, and very quietly clambered back down.

"Two men there," he whispered. "Sound asleep. It's too dark to see far inside but there's a smell of smoke. I'd say they're camping there. Who in the world are they? And how did they get here, and why?"

"I can't think," said Tom, puzzled. "Unless . . . unless they've stolen all these plans and documents, got a boat in the night, came here, and are waiting for someone to fetch the case. Waiting to hand everything over for payment."

"It could be that," said Andy. "Anyway, I think we should pick up all the papers we can see, stuff them into the case and take it away with us. There's something very peculiar about the whole thing. We'd better be quick, though. Those men may wake up at any minute."

The four children began to stuff the papers into the case as fast as they could. But before they could finish picking up every one, they heard the sound of voices from the cave above.

"Quick!" said Tom, shutting the case in a hurry. "We'd better take this and go. They'll be out in a minute. If we keep behind this hill we can get down to the ridge of rocks without being seen."

They set off as quietly as they could, Andy and Tom carrying the suitcase between them. It wasn't really very heavy because it only held papers. They hurried as much as possible over the uneven ground and through the bracken, and came to the rocky ridge.

"Get to the other side, then if the men come out of the cave and look round they won't see us," said Andy. So down they clambered to the east side of the ridge and kept out of sight as they made their way to the channel between the rocks.

But there they had a setback. How were they going to get the suitcase across the channel without soaking the papers inside and probably destroying them? That was a puzzle! They couldn't risk wetting the papers – they might be quite priceless.

"Look here, I've got an idea," said Andy at last. "Let's hide the suitcase somewhere here. Then I'll swim across by myself, go along the ridge on the other side, make my way to the *Andy*, and push her off on the water. I'll sail her along the channel to here, and you can all get into her as I pass. You can chuck the suitcase down to the deck. It won't hurt it, and if it bursts open again, well, we must just see that the wind doesn't get the papers!"

"Good idea," said Tom. "You go off now, Andy, and get the boat. We'll hide the suitcase somewhere near and wait for you."

Andy slid into the water, and they watched him swim swiftly across the little channel. He clambered out on the other side, waved to them, and then went across the rocks to the mainland. He disappeared, and the others sat down and looked at one another.

"Suppose those men go looking for the suitcase and find us?" said Pippa fearfully. "What do we say?"

"We just say we're picnicking here for the day," said Tom. "And we'll say we're being picked up by somebody later. That's perfectly true, but the men may think that a boat has dropped us here for the day and will fetch us this evening."

"I see. So they won't guess we've already got a boat here and are going off in it – with the papers," said Pippa. "I do wish we hadn't got to stick on this island because of the suitcase. I'd feel much safer on the other one!"

"So would I," said Zoe. "I don't know why we didn't go with Andy, except that I don't want to leave Tom on his own."

"I wouldn't have minded," said Tom. "Look out – I can hear the men. They sound pretty angry!"

Sure enough, the two men appeared in the distance, and the children cowered behind a rock. "We haven't hidden the suitcase yet. We *are* idiots," whispered Tom. He pulled it nearer to him and looked round desperately for a hiding place.

"Look, there's a hole under this rock," whispered Pippa. "It would just about take the case. Shove it under, and I'll pull off some seaweed and drape it over the hole to hide the case."

Tom pushed the case into the hole quickly, and the girls pulled seaweed from the rocks around and began to drape it so that the hole and the suitcase were well hidden.

Pippa sat with her legs dangling over it, and her heart began to beat quickly as she heard the voices of the men coming nearer.

"They've seen us!" said Tom. "They'll yell in a minute."

He was right. The men suddenly caught sight of them and stopped in astonishment. "Hey! You children! What in the world are you doing here?" shouted one of the men.

"Hello! We're here picnicking for the day!" yelled Tom, waving as if he were pleased to see them. "Are you? This is a nice island, isn't it?"

The two men came right up to the

children. They looked wary and suspicious. "Look here," said the man who hadn't spoken before, who had a beard and looked rather fierce. "Look here! We've lost a suitcase. Have you seen one?"

"A suitcase! What a funny thing to lose on an island like this," said Pippa, with a laugh. "I expect it's blown out to sea – with the papers!" Too late she realised that she shouldn't have mentioned the papers, and went bright red.

"What papers?" snapped the first man suspiciously. "Did you see any?"

"Oh, yes – they were blowing about all

over the place," said Zoe quickly, sounding as casual as she could. "Heaps of them. I expect there are plenty scattered over the island still. They can't all have blown out to sea!"

The bearded man turned to his friend. "How did the case get open? And where is it now?" he demanded loudly. "I told you to take good care of it. I told you not to let it out of your sight."

"I didn't," pleaded the other man. "Honest, I didn't. I even went to sleep on top of it."

"Sleep! You were supposed to be keeping watch. A fine look-out you are! You must have let it fall down from the entrance while you were dozing!"

"If I did, I couldn't help it – I'm worn out!" moaned the other man, whose chubby face did look pale with dark rings round his eyes. "I haven't had a proper sleep for days."

The man with the beard turned back to the children again. "How did you get here? By boat?"

"Oh yes, of course," said Tom. "But we've got to wait till we're picked up again."

"I see. I suppose the boat dropped you here this morning, and will pick you up this evening," said the first man.

"When are you going?" asked Pippa innocently. "Is a boat coming to pick you up, too? Did you come to watch the birds or something?"

"Er – yes, yes – we're birdwatchers," said the fatter man hurriedly. "We – er – we had a suitcase full of papers about birds – notes, you know – and we're upset to find our case gone, and the papers, too. We'll have to look over the island and pick up all we can. Er – what part of the island is your boat picking you up from?"

"Look, there's a paper!" cried Tom, anxious to get away from the subject of boats. The men turned and saw a piece in the distance. One ran to get it. The other joined him and they looked at it, nodding. They talked together for a while, and then came back to the children, looking stern.

"Now, look here," said the bearded man sternly. "We're not satisfied with what you've told us. We think you've got that suitcase somewhere – and what is more we think you may have a boat hidden away in

41

some cove or other. Tell us the truth and we'll let you go – if not, well, we'll find your boat, scuttle her, and leave you here on this deserted island by yourselves, with no way of getting home!"

"All right," said Tom boldly, "if you think we're thieves, and aren't telling the truth, you look for the suitcase and hunt in every cove of this island for our boat. Then you'll see for yourself."

"We will," said the bearded man, getting angry. He turned to his friend. "Stay here, Fred, and watch these kids," he said. "I'm going all over the island to see if I can find where they've put the case and I'm going to look for their boat, too. That'll be the end of it if I find it!"

"I'll watch the kids," said the other man grimly, and he sat down nearby.

Tom winked at the two frightened girls. The men didn't for one moment imagine that their boat was on the next island, not on this one – nor did they dream that the suitcase was at that moment under Pippa's dangling legs! But, oh dear, how Tom hoped that Andy didn't come too soon with the boat!

CHAPTER FOUR

HOOKED IN MY OWN BOAT!

The bearded man went off to look for the suitcase and the boat. On the way the children saw him bend down to pick up one or two more papers. "We must have missed those," they thought. "Blow!"

Tom got up and clambered up and down the rocks. Zoe joined him. But Pippa sat still, feeling that if she didn't sit on the seaweed that dangled down over the hidden suitcase, it might slip and expose it! That would be dreadful.

"By the way," said Tom, going up to the man who was watching them, the one called Fred, "you said you were birdwatchers, didn't you? Have you seen that lovely cormopetrel? And did you notice all the kittygillies? Lovely, aren't they?"

The girls knew that Tom was making up these bird names, but the man didn't. He nodded surlily. "Yes, lovely birds."

"Where did you say your boat was?" asked Tom, beginning to enjoy himself. "Or did somebody drop you here? And is somebody coming to fetch you? If not, we could give you a lift home ourselves."

The man scowled. "Keep your mouth shut," he said. "I'm not talking to silly kids like you. You tell me where your boat is and I'll tell you where mine is."

"Can't tell you that if I'm to keep my mouth shut!" said Tom. "Anyway, your friend will soon tell you if he finds our boat."

It seemed a long time till the bearded man came back. He must have walked over the tiny island two or three times, hunting here and there, and he had also walked all round the beaches and examined every little inlet to see if he could find a boat.

When at last he came towards them once more the children saw that he had picked up quite a few papers. He shook his head as he came up to the first man.

"No boat," he said. "I've looked in every cove. They told the truth – their boat is nowhere on this island. They must be going to be picked up tonight, like they said. I haven't found the suitcase either."

"Perhaps one of those big gulls carried it off," said Pippa innocently, pointing to where an enormous gull glided with widespread wings over their heads.

"Pah!" said the man. "Well, let me tell you this, you kids – if you've taken that suitcase of ours, we shall know it. We shall be on the watch for your boat tonight, and if we see you going down to it with a suitcase, you'll be very, very sorry. Fred, go up to that hilltop there and keep watch. You can see all round the island from there and you'd see a boat coming in miles away. The mainland is over there – keep a strict watch in that direction and all round too."

The other man nodded. He got up and walked to the hill the bearded man pointed out. It was in the middle of the island and was very high. He sat himself down on the top. The bearded man gave the three children one of his best scowls, and went off, apparently to look for more blown-about papers.

"He won't find many more," whispered Tom. "We picked up almost all there were! Gosh, if only he knew that Pippa is sitting practically on top of his precious suitcase!"

"Don't!" said Pippa. "I felt as if he must see it through my legs and the seaweed every time he looked in my direction."

"What do we do now?" asked Zoe. "Wait for Andy? That man up on the hill will spot the red sail as soon as the *Andy* comes round."

"If only we could tell Andy not to put it up!" said Tom. "If he rowed round he might not be seen. Those rocks would hide him, and I don't think that fellow up there can see right down to where we are. I'm pretty sure he can't see the channel."

"Andy's taking a jolly long time," said Zoe. "I feel rather worried about him. Surely he should be here by now?"

"Yes, he should," said Tom. "I'm just wondering if he's found that he can't shove the boat off. It might have sunk down into the sand or something. Anyway, the tide was coming in so he might be able to get it on the water then. We can only wait. Oh, I say! I've just thought of something!"

"What?" said the two girls eagerly.

"This," said Tom, producing the plastic

bag he had brought. "The chocolate! You could do with it now, I bet! Or do you still feel you can't eat anything, Pippa?"

"I'm starving hungry," said Pippa. "Thank goodness you brought the chocolate. I expect it's all squishy and smells of plastic, but I shan't mind!"

It was squishy, and it did smell of plastic, but certainly no one minded. They ate it all except for a piece they kept for Andy.

"I wonder what the time is," said Pippa at last. "The sun's going down. I do wish Andy would come. I suppose you couldn't slip into the water, swim across the channel and go and find Andy, could you, Tom? He might have had an accident, or something."

Tom considered. "No, I don't think I'd better do that. If that fellow up there saw me, I'd give the game away properly. He'd guess our boat was on the next island if he spotted me swimming across. But I'll go when it's a bit darker."

"Let's play catch or something," said Zoe. "I'm getting a bit cold in my swimming things. It'll warm us up!"

So they played rather a dangerous game of catch on the rocks. Still, it warmed them up. By the time they were tired of it the sun was just disappearing.

"Now it will soon get dark," said Pippa. "Hello! Here's Mr Beard again!"

So it was. He came up to the children. "It looks as if your boat isn't coming for you," he said. "What do you suppose has happened? Weren't they going to pick you up in daylight?"

"I can't imagine what's happened!" said Tom truthfully. "What about your boat? Is it coming at night? A motor-boat, perhaps?"

The bearded man didn't answer. He joined the other man on the hill, and they talked earnestly together.

"Look!" Tom suddenly gave the girls a nudge. "Our boat! The sail isn't up, thank goodness! Andy's rowing."

"They won't see him now, it's getting too dark," said Pippa. "What about the suitcase? Shall we get it out?"

"No, not till the boat is exactly in the middle of the channel. Then we'll drag out the case and drop it, plonk, on the deck," said Tom. "I'll do that. You two girls go down to the lowest rock now, ready to dive in and swim to the boat."

Pippa and Zoe went down to the lowest rocks and waited, trembling with excitement. They could just make out the two men sitting on the high, rocky hill. Andy and the boat came nearer and nearer. How the children hoped he would not hail them! But he didn't. He rowed carefully into the channel and at once spotted the two girls. They dived in cleanly and swam the few strokes to the boat.

And at that moment one of the men gave a loud shout. "What's that? Look, it's a boat! A rowing boat! Where did it come from? Quick, those children will be away in it. Stop it! We must stop it!"

Andy pulled the two girls into the boat, and then worked it as near to the rocks as he could without danger. He could see Tom dragging the suitcase out from under the seaweedy rock.

"Quick," he called. "They're coming! Quick, Tom!"

Poor Tom was being as quick as he could but the suitcase had swollen a little with the damp under the rock, and was now jammed fast. He tugged and tugged, hearing the shouts and the running footsteps coming nearer and nearer. Would the suitcase never come out?

At last it came free but with such a rush that Tom fell down on to the rocks below and almost rolled into the water. He clutched at a handful of seaweed and saved himself. The suitcase slid on top of him. He rolled over, got up, snatched at the handle and went as quickly as he dared over the slippery rocks.

A big stone came whizzing near his head. He ducked. Goodness! The men were throwing bits of rock and stones at him! Another stone hit the suitcase, and then one glanced off his ankle, making him wince.

"Quickly, Tom," shrieked Pippa. "He's coming for you!"

Tom glanced round and saw the man with the beard bend down to pick up a lump of jagged rock. Above him, the other man was puffing up the cliff towards the cave. What was he up to?

"Chuck it," shouted a voice from below.

It was Andy. "Heave in the suitcase," he called up, "I'm just here – I'm near enough for you to jump in, too. Come *on*, Tom!"

Tom saw the boat just below him. With a mighty effort he took hold of the suitcase and threw it down to the boat. It landed with such force that it almost knocked Andy over. The girls pulled it quickly to one side and waited for Tom to jump in, too.

But in his panic Tom missed his footing and fell between the boat and the rocks. He spluttered and gasped and grabbed at the side of the boat. Andy caught hold of him and hauled him in. A large piece of rock bounced on deck and the girls screamed.

Andy seized the oars and rowed for dear life. The bearded man clambered swiftly down the rocks and came to the edge of the channel. But the boat had slid out of it now and was making for the open sea. He raised his arm, took careful aim and sent the rock hurtling towards the boat.

"Duck!" shouted Zoe as the rock missed them by centimetres and splashed into the water on the other side.

"Don't panic," said Andy, pulling at the oars with all his might. "We'll soon be out of range. He's a good shot, but not that good."

"What about the other one?" asked Tom, kneeling in the bottom of the boat rubbing his ankle. "Where's he?"

"He ran away," said Pippa. "Up into the cave. Don't ask me why."

"There he is now," panted Andy between strokes.

The others turned to look and saw Fred at the mouth of the cave. He was laden down with what he'd been to fetch from inside. Under one arm he was carrying a stubby tube on legs, out of the top of which stuck a short cylinder with a conical hat. In the other hand he grasped the handle of a square wooden box.

The man with the beard had clambered up to meet him and together they hurried to the edge of the rocks. There they pulled out the two front legs of the tube and stood it up like a small easel. Fred wrenched the top off the wooden box and reached inside. In one hand he pulled out what looked like a small anchor made from three huge fishing hooks joined together. This was tied to the end of a coil of rope in his other hand.

Fred pulled a few metres of rope from

the box. The man with the beard grabbed the three-hooked "anchor" and slotted it into the side of cylinder which was now pointing upwards and out to sea – out towards the retreating boat.

"They've got a rocket," grunted Andy, burying the oars deeper and tugging harder

than ever. "The coastguards use them to rescue sailors when their ships are wrecked, but I think our friends have got other ideas."

"Do you mean they want to sink us?" asked Pippa in alarm.

"Not sink us," said Andy. "Catch us maybe, with that grappling hook of theirs."

"The sail! Put up the sail!" shouted Tom. "Pippa, Zoe, help me while Andy rows. We can still do it."

The three worked desperately at the ropes. The sail unfolded. It went up – it shook out and the wind immediately filled it! Andy shipped the oars with relief and reached for the tiller. The *Andy* seemed to sense their danger and lifted her bows higher out of the water as she tried to speed away from the two men on the rocks.

"Get your heads down," said Andy urgently. "They could fire that thing at us at any moment."

Pippa, Zoe and Tom huddled down in the bottom of the boat beside the suitcase. Pressing their heads against the side they heard the water rushing past the *Andy's* sleek hull. Looking up, they saw the red sail straining against the boom and the little flag fluttering madly at the top of the mast.

Suddenly there was a terrifying explosion and a rushing noise that grew louder as it got closer. The children saw a flash of flame roar over them trailing a long tail. Then came a splash on the other side of the boat followed a second or two later by a thud right on top of them.

"Help me with this rope," shouted Andy. "They've fired it right through the rigging. We must get rid of it before the grappling hook catches hold."

Everything had happened so quickly that Tom and the twins were in a daze. Thank goodness Andy still had his wits about him! When they stood up they saw him tugging at a stout rope that was hanging from the top of the mast. The rope stretched over the side, into the water and snaked back to the rocks where the two men were tying it securely round a large boulder.

As the children watched the rope grew straighter and tighter until it suddenly sprang out of the water. At the same moment the *Andy* lurched to one side and came to a dead stop.

"Watch out!" yelled Andy as everyone on board was thrown off their feet. Down in the cabin, bottles, tins, plates, knives, forks, cups and the contents of the picnic basket crashed to the floor.

Andy had nearly been thrown over the side as the rope was snatched from his hands. Tom fell heavily against the cabin roof and lay winded. Pippa sprawled over the suitcase. And Zoe was rubbing the side of her head where a large lump was starting to form.

Slowly, the boat came level once again. The rope now stretched tight from the mast, above their heads. The strange "anchor" with its three hooks was snagged in the rigging. It had torn a hole through the red sail.

"What's happening?" exclaimed Pippa. "Why have we stopped?"

"They've caught us with their grappling hook," said Andy. "They fired the rocket over us so that it would catch the rigging. Now all they have to do is to pull in the rope. A fine fisherman I am," he added bitterly, "hooked in my own boat."

"Let's cut the rope," suggested Tom. But even he could see that was hopeless when he got to his feet. They had no knife to hand and even if they had the rope was too high to reach.

Already the two men were hauling on it and slowly the *Andy* was giving up the struggle. As the children watched help-lessly, the distance between them and the shore began to grow smaller. Metre by metre the two men pulled the boat towards them until its sides bumped against the rocks.

"You thought you could get away, did you?" sneered the man with the beard. Fred was red in the face and too puffed to speak.

"Now we've got all of you. We've got your boat. *And* we've got our suitcase back," gloated the bearded man. "You would have saved yourselves a lot of trouble if you had given it to us in the first place. And now we have to decide what we are going to do with four interfering children. Best to sink their boat and shut them up, don't you think?" he asked Fred, who was slumped on a rock, mopping his face with a handkerchief.

"Leave it to Mr Brown," he panted. "Let him decide. We've only got a few hours to wait before we bring him back here."

"Maybe you're right," said the bearded man. "It's getting dark and they can't cause any more trouble now. Get out, you lot," he ordered the children. "And do as you're told if you know what's good for you."

"I'm getting cold," shivered Tom.

"Get your clothes on then and come up here," snapped Fred, who was starting to rub his arms to stay warm. "And hurry up about it."

The children needed no urging. A chill breeze had picked up from the sea and they were glad to pull on something warm to keep out the night air.

"I can't find my jersey," said Andy. "It must be in the cabin."

"Well, get it," answered the bearded man crossly, "and hurry up. You've wasted enough of our time as it is."

Andy did as he was told and soon the four children were huddled together on the rocks, looking at their boat bobbing empty and alone below them.

"Take them up to the cave," said the man

with the beard, and pointed to the boat. "I'll take care of this," he went on.

"Don't you do anything to my boat!" Andy told him angrily.

"Oh, I shan't," answered the bearded man with a nasty chuckle. "It could be useful, after all. Now, go up to the cave before I make you."

Zoe led the way quickly, followed by Andy, Pippa and Tom. Fred brought up the rear. There wasn't a proper path. They had to pick their way through the bracken and sometimes stubbed their toes on rocks hidden beneath.

"More to the left," puffed Fred, who wasn't enjoying the climb one little bit. Zoe lifted her eyes and saw a dull glow above them in that direction. It was the mouth of the cave. Her head was throbbing and she was hungry. She took a deep breath and moved off again.

Down below there was just enough light to show the man with the beard tying the *Andy* to two big rocks by the channel. What were they going to do with it? And why was the boat going to be "useful after all"?

None of them had any idea.

CHAPTER FIVE

THE MYSTERY DEEPENS

After climbing through the rough bracken in the cold, the cave was warm and welcoming.

The glow that Pippa had seen came from a low fire, built on one side of the cave. Above it, a natural chimney took the smoke up through a split in the rock. The only light came from the fire, so the cave and its contents were cast in heavy shadows.

"Move inside so I can light the lamp," Fred told them. Zoe edged forward, holding her hands in front of her, feeling along the rough rock wall to guide her way. Pippa followed her sister, lightly touching her shoulder.

"Drat it!" exclaimed Tom, who thought he could find his own way and had tripped on the uneven surface, crashing on to his knees.

"Steady now," said Andy at his side, reaching down to help him up. "We're in no hurry. Mind how you go."

"Thanks, Andy," said Tom, feeling rather stupid.

The older boy stood up again and as he did so his head brushed against something soft and heavy.

"Come on, you lot, keep moving," said Fred. "Don't let all the warmth out."

Behind them the children could hear him scrabbling about at one side of the cave. With a grunt of satisfaction he seemed to find what he was looking for. More scrabbling followed and then there was a dull thud and a puff of cold air.

"That's better," muttered Fred, sounding more cheerful than they had heard him all afternoon. He struck a match and in its light they could see him lift the glass on an oil lamp and light the wick. The glass dropped back with a click and the cave started to fill with a warm golden light as Fred adjusted the flame.

It took a moment for their eyes to get used to the light. When they did so, they saw that the mouth of the cave had disappeared. At least, the last faint light on the sea had. The entrance of the cave was now pitch black. The breeze had gone too.

"Don't touch my fire," grumbled Fred when Zoe picked up a stick from a pile and went to poke the flames into life. "That's got to last me all night. And that plane is as cold as the grave," he muttered to himself.

While Fred stoked the fire Andy took a few steps backwards towards the mouth of the cave, with one hand reaching behind him. His fingers brushed up against a coarse material. He knew the feel of it immediately. It was heavy material which would stop light spilling out into the night sky where it might be seen. But why was there a black-out curtain in this isolated cave? What was the secret it was hiding?

The mysterious papers. The suitcase. The two men who had taken them prisoner and taken his boat. A picture was falling into place in Andy's mind and he didn't like it one little bit.

"I'm hungry," grumbled Tom. "We're all hungry. If you're going to keep us here, the least you can do is give us something to eat."

"Something hot, please," added Zoe, who was crouching over the fire. "I'm freezing."

"It's lucky for you we won't be needing all this stuff," answered Fred. "You can keep this island, and all these birds. Nothing but noise and mess, that's all they make from dawn till dusk. Still, you'll find that out for yourselves soon enough, when we're gone," he said with a chuckle.

"There's the kettle. There's the water. And there's the stores. If you're so desperate for something hot, you can make a nice pot of tea. My mug's that big one," he said, slumping on to an upturned box.

Pippa unhooked the smoky kettle from a chain hanging over the fire and filled it with water from a barrel standing nearby. Doing it reminded her of summer camps, except that those were always full of light and laughter. This cave couldn't have been more different.

"I can't see a thing over here," said Tom, who was peering into boxes and sacks at the back of the cave. "Haven't you got another light?"

"Blooming kids," muttered Fred, getting

to his feet. He found another oil lamp, lit it and walked towards the back of the cave where he hung it on a hook above Tom's head.

"That's better," said Tom, whose eyes had just spotted a huge slab of chocolate in one of the boxes. But a sudden fluttering at his back made him jump round with a start. Behind, in some sort of cage, eight small beady eyes twinkled at him in the lamplight, moving close together and then apart. For a moment Tom thought he was looking at some monster of the deep that had taken to living in a cave. Then there came a familiar cooing sound and the monster instantly turned into the heads of four pigeons. Could one of them be the pigeon they'd seen earlier in the day?

"Here, what are you doing with those birds?" shouted Fred, who looked as startled as Tom. "You come away from them right now!"

"I was only trying to find the tea things . . ." began Tom.

"What are they doing here?" asked Pippa. "Why have you got pigeons caged up in a cave like this?"

"Eggs," said Fred, not very convincingly. "They – er – lay – er – very good eggs. Better than hens' eggs, if you ask me. Now, you leave them alone. Get out of the way and let me find the tea."

Tom moved aside to let him pass, but not before he had taken another quick look at the pigeons. There was something about them that made him think they weren't just ordinary pigeons. One thing he was sure about – they hadn't been brought all the way out to this island just to lay eggs for Fred and the man with the beard.

Fred took the lamp from its hook and held it above the boxes while he poked about inside them. Out came a box of tea, a bag of sugar and a tin of condensed milk. From another box he pulled out a teapot and two mugs.

"You'll have to share," he said, handing the mugs to Pippa. "We weren't expecting visitors, you understand," he went on, putting on a posh voice. No one laughed.

"Haven't you got anything to eat?" continued Tom, remembering the chocolate he had sccn.

"Take your pick," said Fred. "Bird food

or biscuits, that's all I'm giving you."

"I'd like a biscuit, please," said Zoe, trying to remember her manners even to a horrid man like Fred.

"Here you are then," he said, reaching inside a sack and pulling out four big hard biscuits the size of saucers and as thick as crumpets. "Those should keep you quiet for a while."

"Ugh! They don't taste like any biscuit I've ever eaten," exclaimed Pippa after she'd tried to take a bite from hers.

"They're ships' biscuits," said Andy. "Dad says that's what they used to live on when he was a sailor – those and salted meat."

"They're more like dog biscuits, if you ask me," commented Tom, though he kept on chewing.

"Honestly, Tom, you'd eat anything!" said Pippa.

"Anything's better than nothing," answered her brother, gnawing at the tough biscuit like a dog at a bone.

Zoe was more interested in having something hot to drink. While the other three struggled to get their teeth working on their biscuits, she put a little hot water into the teapot to warm it, then spooned in the tea and put on the lid. Then she pulled the cuffs of her jersey down over her hands so that she could hold the piping hot teapot against her chest to get warm.

"Do your pigeons lay big eggs?" Tom asked Fred innocently.

"Quite big," answered Fred.

"As big as a kittigilly's?"

"Yes, as big as that. Not that it's any of your business."

"They must make a good meal then, if they're twice as big as a hen's egg," said Tom. He was enjoying himself. Fred was not. He scowled at Tom, and didn't reply. Instead he turned to Zoe.

"Are you going to be all night making that tea?" he asked her crossly. "Three sugars for me, I like mine sweet."

"Would you like some milk?" asked Pippa politely, holding the can of condensed milk over Fred's mug.

"Not too much, I can't stand the stuff," grumbled Fred. "Why couldn't Mr Brown leave us with some decent grub, that's what I want to know?"

"Have you been here a long time, then?" inquired Pippa, handing Fred his tea and offering him a spoon to stir it.

"Longer than I wanted," replied Fred, taking a sip from the steaming mug.

"You've enough food and provisions to last a good few weeks," commented Andy, who had been quietly observing the layout of the cave while Fred's attention had been distracted by the others.

"Yeah, well, we're not staying that long. But you should be pleased, because the way things look, you'll be needing the food. You're going to be here a while yet. That's what you get from sticking your nose into other people's business."

"Whose business is that?" asked Zoe, offering the teapot to top up Fred's mug. "Mr Brown's? He sounds very important."

"Oh, he is – he is important – he's—"

"—He's too important for idle chatter," snapped a voice from the entrance of the cave.

They all looked round and peered into the shadows where the bearded man was standing, glaring at Fred.

"Mr Brown's so important, he can make

people hold their tongues for a long time, a very long time. You'd better remember that, all of you." He was looking straight at Fred as he said this.

"Would you like some tea?" asked Pippa, trying to sound cheerful. "It's freshly made."

"Black, no sugar, no milk," ordered the bearded man curtly.

He snatched the mug without a word, kicked Fred on the ankle and indicated with his head that he wanted to speak to him in private.

The two men disappeared into the shadows right to the back of the cave where the children could only catch snatches of

their muffled conversation. Occasional words, "boat", "kids", "tonight", "box", "suitcase", reached them, but how they fitted together and what the men were planning remained a mystery.

"More tea, anyone?" asked Pippa, who had refilled the teapot from the kettle.

"Yes, please," said Tom. "If you stick these biscuits in and make them soggy, they don't taste quite as bad."

"What would your mother say if she saw you doing that?" said Andy, grinning.

"Well, I do it at school and she doesn't know about that, but even the food at school's better than this," admitted Tom.

"It's good to feel warmer," said Zoe.

"How's your head?" asked Andy. "You took quite a bang when the *Andy* went over."

"Better now," replied Zoe. "It'll be fine in the morning."

"I wonder how long we're going to be trapped here?" whispered Pippa.

"That's what they're talking about now," said Tom. "By the sound of it we could be stuck on this island for ages. Will your father come looking for us, Andy?"

"After the last time, he will," replied Andy, "but with so many islands it could take days to find us and by then our friends will be long gone, and they won't be leaving the *Andy* for us to sail home in, you can be sure of that."

The sound of footsteps from the back of the cave silenced their whispers.

"Do you want more tea?" Pippa asked once more as the men returned to the fire.

"No," said the bearded man gruffly. "And don't give him any either. I don't want him getting too cosy. We've got work to do tonight and he'll need all his wits about him making sure you lot don't cause us any more trouble."

"Why? Are you going somewhere?" asked Tom.

"That's none of your business," said the man with the beard.

"You're *not* taking my boat!" Andy told him firmly.

"Huh!" scoffed the bearded man, "I can just imagine what Mr Brown would say if I turned up in that. But don't worry, sonny, you won't be using it either. Fred is going to make sure about that, aren't you, Fred?"

and he gave his nastiest smile as he spoke.

"Now listen here, you lot," began Fred, trying to sound fierce. "There's no way you're going to get off this island without your precious boat, and we'll be taking good care of that. You failed once and we're not giving you a second chance. Be good little children. Wait here patiently and I'm sure some kind person will find you, sooner or later. But if you try anything on while we're around, you won't get a second chance at that either. I'm warning you."

"Time to get things started," interrupted the bearded man, who had sat down on a wooden box and was writing something in pencil on a small piece of paper.

"Get me the darkest coloured one," he told Fred. "There's no moon tonight, so we may as well make the most of it."

The four children watched as Fred made his way to the cage which held the pigeons. He unlatched the wire door, reached inside and lifted out a dark grey bird, the colour of stormclouds.

"Here," he mumbled, handing it to the bearded man.

With surprising gentleness the man with

the beard took the pigeon in both hands
and ran his fingers lightly down its neck.
Then, holding it in one hand, he slid what
looked like a tiny cigarette into a very small
cylinder attached by a ring to one of the
pigeon's legs.

Giving the bird another stroke, he got to
his feet and walked to the mouth of the
cave.

"Time check," he barked at Fred.

"Nine fifty-nine," answered Fred, holding his wrist close to the lamp so that he
could peer intently at his watch. "Ten, nine,
eight, seven, six, five, four, three, two, one

73

. . . Ten o'clock precisely," he announced.

The man with the beard drew back the black-out curtain, held the pigeon outside and let it go. There was a hasty beating of wings and then silence as the bird disappeared into the dark sky on its mysterious flight. Where could it be going at that time of night?

"At least we got that part right," said the bearded man, letting the curtain fall back in place. "We'd better get ready for our big bird," he said to Fred. "You bring the fuel, I'll bring the lights, and this." Reaching inside a box, he lifted out a cylinder with a conical hat – another rocket!

Fred obeyed without a word. From another of the wooden boxes he lifted a petrol can and a metal funnel. The man with the beard picked up a big torch and switched it on. Its powerful beam swung round the cave and stopped on the box of matches Fred had used to light the oil lamps.

"Take those too," said the bearded man. "We don't want any little eyes looking into things that don't concern them, do we?"

Then he went to the oil lamp over the

stores, lifted it from the hook, raised the glass and blew out the flame.

"You aren't going to leave us alone in the dark?" cried Pippa, trying to sound helpless and scared, though she didn't really mind the dark at all.

"You've got the fire. That's all you need," was the answer, and with another puff the second oil lamp was blown out too.

The cave was plunged into darkness except for the glow from the cooking fire.

"Remember, we'll be watching. If we see a chink of light showing from this curtain, you'll be for it," the bearded man's voice snarled from behind the torch beam which was shining right in the children's eyes. "Don't any of you budge till we get back," and with that the torchlight swung away and moved towards the curtain, the two oil lamps clinking together as they were carried off.

There was a small gust of cold air from outside and then the sound of footsteps moving away down the cliff. Zoe, Pippa, Tom and Andy stood looking at each other in the firelight.

CHAPTER SIX

SECRETS OF THE CAVE

It was Andy who broke the silence. "There's something very fishy going on," he said, half to himself.

"You can say that again," said Pippa. "Whatever those two men are doing they're up to no good, I'll be bound."

"But what are they doing?" asked Zoe. "I'm totally confused."

"What's so special about this rotten old cave?" chimed in Tom. "And why don't they want us to know what they're getting up to? It's pitch black outside. This island's miles from anywhere, so no one can see what's happening. Why are they being so secretive?"

"Don't forget that an aircraft could spot even a small light," commented Andy. "What do you think that thick curtain's for? Then there are fishing boats. We saw those marker flags, remember. Someone must come here to check their pots for lobsters and crabs. They might notice people on the island. Those two men don't want to be discovered, that's why they're being so careful to keep us out of the way."

"And to keep themselves hidden," added Pippa.

"Anyway, they've gone for the moment," said Tom, who had felt his way towards the pile of stores. "I saw a huge bar of chocolate in here somewhere and I'm famished."

"Won't they be cross when they find we've eaten it?" asked Zoe.

"The one called Fred said it was lucky for us that there was still something left to eat," answered Tom.

"Aye, that's right," Andy remembered. "So it sounds as if they won't be needing to eat it themselves."

"Do you mean they really are going to leave us trapped in a cave on a deserted island?" said Pippa.

"It looks very like it," Andy replied. "They've obviously got something in mind for the *Andy*. Maybe they're going to sail off in her tonight, leaving us bchind until someone finds us."

"And they'll have disappeared by then," said Tom, "and no one will have a chance of catching them and finding out what they're really up to."

"Aren't we forgetting something?" said Zoe, who had been trying to blow the flames into life and was now standing up.

"What?" asked the others.

"If those two men were going to leave the island by themselves, they'd need a boat of their own, wouldn't they? We didn't see one when we were looking round. And they couldn't have known that we would be coming in our boat. So they must have planned to leave in another way."

"You're right," said Tom. "They told us they were going to be picked up by a boat. Maybe that's true. It's obvious that they don't know the first thing about birds. They can't be birdwatchers, but there might be a boat to come and collect them after all."

"It's possible," agreed Andy. "I can't see how they could leave the island any other way. But you saw how tricky it was sailing through the narrow channel in daylight. Coming in at night would be even more difficult. I shouldn't want to risk it."

A silence followed as they each thought through what had been said. Andy was right about trying to land a boat at night. But the two men must have been expecting something to happen soon. Why else would they have gone out in the dark with lights, warning the children not to follow them?

"What do you suppose they were doing with that pigeon?" Tom wanted to know.

"They made sure that it was released right on ten o'clock," Pippa reminded them. "So it can't be flying just anywhere. Someone must be expecting it to arrive at a certain time."

"Which means that there's something extra specially important about it. I knew they weren't just any old pigeons," said Tom.

"It's carrying a message!" exclaimed Zoe suddenly. "That's what it's doing. We saw the man with the beard writing something. He must have folded up the paper with the message and attached it to the pigeon's leg."

"Carrier pigeons," whistled Andy. "Very clever – very, very clever. No radio signals to track, no flashing lights to give them away, just a wee bird flying along minding its own business. Who's going to think there's anything suspicious about that?"

"Who do you think it's taking the message to?" asked Pippa.

"I bet it's that person they call Mr Brown," Andy answered. "They talked about seeing him in a few hours."

"Didn't they say they were going to be bringing him back here?" cut in Zoe.

"Yes! You're right! That's just what they did say," exclaimed Andy. "Somehow or other they're going to be leaving the island soon, and then returning. But why? Unless it's to pack up everything here and disappear for good. Maybe they want to keep us prisoner until they've made their getaway."

"If that's right, it means they must've finished what they came to do," Zoe continued. "It must have something to do with those papers in the suitcase; the plans or codes or whatever they are. We were right to try to get away with them. They must be terribly secret and important for the men to go to all this trouble."

"Someone has spent a lot of time

planning this," remarked Andy. "Carrier pigeons, stores of food, the rocket-fired grappling hook – you don't take those on a normal birdwatching trip!"

"That hook thing with the rocket puzzles me," said Pippa. "They couldn't have brought that just to catch the *Andy*. It must be needed for something special, but I can't imagine what."

"Neither can I," said Andy thoughtfully. "Neither can I."

"Found it!" shouted Tom in triumph. "I knew it was in one of these boxes. There's lots of stuff in bags, but it needs cooking. This doesn't and I bet it's nicer than those dog biscuit things."

"Sea-dog biscuits," said Pippa with a laugh.

Tom made his way through the shadows back to the fireside where the others crouched round the low flames to see what he'd found.

It was a huge bar of chocolate, just as he'd said. But it wasn't a type of chocolate they recognized. The name was different and the printing on the back was in a foreign language.

"Wow! Look at this!" shouted Tom. "This must have come here with the men – which means they must be in the pay of a foreign country!"

"We must try to get home so that we can tell the police about the suitcase," said Andy, breaking off a chunk from the thick brown slab and popping it into his mouth.

"Do you think they're spies?" asked Pippa.

"Spies or secret agents. If they've got food from a foreign country, they must be working for it and that makes them enemies of our country," said Andy, passing the chocolate bar to Zoe, who snapped off another piece and munched it hungrily.

"I wish there was more light," said Tom, between mouthfuls. "I wouldn't mind having a good look round this cave to see what else they've hidden in here."

"That's why they took the lamps and the matches," replied Pippa.

"Well done, brainbox! D'you think I didn't know that?" snapped back Tom.

"Steady on, you two," Andy told them. "Let's see if we can get more light from the fire. Tom's right. We should try to find out if there's anything else the police should know about."

"Did you find any fat, Tom, when you were looking for the chocolate?" asked Zoe.

"I might have done," said Tom. "You can't see much over there, but there was some greasy paper wrapped round a block of something squidgy."

"That sounds promising," said Zoe. "Come on, everyone, let's see if we can find it. If it's what I think it is, we might be able to make a torch."

"Doesn't that need batteries?" asked Tom.

"Not that kind of torch, not an electric one," Pippa told him, trying not to sound clever. "Zoe means an old-fashioned torch like the ones people used in olden days."

"Like in the stories of Robin Hood, you mean," said her brother. "Torches with fire at the end, burning in dark passages and spooky dungeons."

"Those are the ones," said Zoe. "And it would be just right in this cave. I can't think of anywhere more like a spooky dungeon."

All four children made their way through the dark cave to the pile of stores.

They each started feeling the contents of a box until Pippa called out excitedly, "Is this some, Zoe?"

"Let me have it," said Zoe, taking a large block of something from her sister. Holding it in one hand, she unfolded the paper and sniffed the contents.

"Almost," she said. "This is cheese. We need cooking fat – lard. It's very greasy, so it will burn a bit like candle wax. Keep trying."

The search continued.

"This could be what you're after," said Andy a few moments later, handing over a misshapen lump wrapped in greaseproof paper.

"Well done," Zoe answered, carefully carrying the white blob over to the fire. "What we need now is a strong stick and some rags to wrap round it. Anything will do."

"How about a bit of sacking?" suggested Tom. "There are some torn-up pieces over here."

"Just the ticket," said Zoe. "Pippa, can you find that spoon we used for the sugar? We'll need it to spread the lard."

"Here it is," Pippa's voice answered from the shadows.

Meanwhile Andy had selected a good stout stick from the pile of firewood and Tom had brought a bundle of sacking over to the fire.

"Right," said Zoe, taking charge. "Pippa, you hold the lard near the fire, so it gets soft and so I can see it. Andy, you hold the stick and twist it as we wrap the sacking round. Tom, you wind on the sacking while I spread the fat between the layers."

It wasn't the neatest torch ever made and they all got a bit messy with the dust and sand from the sacking, and from the melting lard. But soon there was a thick bandage of sacking covered with fat wrapped tightly round one end of the stick.

"You take it, Zoe," said Andy, handing it to her. "It was your brainwave. You light it."

"I don't know if it will work," said Zoe cautiously, holding the fat bandage just above the glowing embers of the fire.

Soon a tail of thick black smoke began rising from it, followed a moment later by a rich yellow flame. "What a pong!" complained Tom, backing away.

"Never mind," said Andy. "You wanted more light, and now, thanks to Zoe's ingenuity, we've got more light. Now come on, let's make good use of it before the flame dies down."

"What about the men – won't they see it?" asked Pippa anxiously.

"No, they can't, because of the curtain," Andy reassured her. "It stops light shining out. The only way they would notice it is if we pulled back the curtain. We're not going to do that, so there's nothing to worry about."

With Zoe leading the way, holding the flaming torch above her head, the four children began searching the cave. In the light of the flickering flames they poked through the boxes of stores, but found nothing there except tins of fruit, bags of vegetables and some meat that was starting to get a bit smelly. One box was filled with cans of petrol. Zoe kept the flaming torch well away from those. She didn't let it get too close to one of the other boxes either, the one that held the spare rockets. Whatever they were really used for, it wasn't just for stopping escaping boats that

the rockets had been brought to the island.

"Let's try over here," suggested Andy, indicating the very back of the cave where the two men had gone to have their talk out of hearing of the children.

"What's this?" asked Pippa, who had just stumbled over a long metal box.

Zoe brought the torch over for a closer look. Pippa knelt down and undid the clasp holding the lid in place. Then she lifted the lid carefully until they could all see inside. Another object shaped like a rocket lay in metal brackets. It had a red nose, and black tail-fins. Tom was the first to recognise these.

"Hey! Remember one of those pieces of paper we found, one with part of a plan or something on it. Didn't the drawing look just like that?" he said excitedly, pointing his finger at part of a tail-fin.

"Well spotted," Andy congratulated him. "It's like a jigsaw puzzle, but I think you're right, Tom. That's what some of those bits of paper must be – plans for this rocket, or whatever it is."

"I'm glad we found it," said Pippa. "I'm sure the police will want to know all about this – we've got to get off this island and tell them."

"Mmm . . ." said Andy, thinking hard.

Pippa closed and fastened the lid. They were just about to continue their search when they heard the sound of an engine starting up! All four stopped where they were, listening in amazement.

"What on earth can that be?" asked Zoe.

"It sounds like a lawnmower," said Tom.

"Don't be daft. Who'd have a mower out here?"

"I only said it sounds like a lawnmower," said Tom indignantly. "I didn't say it *was* one."

"Is it a boat, Andy?" asked Zoe.

"It could be," said Andy, "but we didn't hear it approaching. That engine started up out of the blue. Unless there was a boat hidden somewhere that we missed, I'd say that engine's on the island itself."

"On the island?" said Pippa in surprise.

"What for?" asked Zoe. "What's the use of an engine if it isn't in a boat?"

"Your guess is as good as mine," said Andy. "And right now I can't even begin to guess what it's used for. But I wouldn't mind betting that it runs on petrol – the petrol stored in those cans over there."

"Wow! Do you think it's some sort of secret weapon?" exclaimed Tom.

"Hardly," said Andy. "Why would anyone want to use a secret weapon out here? There's nothing to use it against. But that thing in the metal box looks very mysterious – that's more likely to be a secret weapon, don't you think? Oh, if only we could get off this island!" he groaned.

"Do you think we should put out the torch, Andy? In case those men come back?" asked Zoe. "It won't be so easy to hear them coming if that engine keeps running."

"Good thinking," said Andy.

"Put it on the fire," suggested Pippa. "That way no one will ever know what we used. It will just burn up and disappear."

"Let me put the lard back first," said Andy. "I'll need the light to see what I'm doing."

"Be quick," Pippa told him. "Those men might come back at any time."

Andy hastily wrapped up the lump of lard and put it back in the box where he had found it. "All right," he called over and Zoe dropped the torch on to the embers of the cooking fire.

The flames leaped up, casting long eerie shadows as the last of the fat and sacking burned away, and then they died down again.

As the crackling of the fire faded a new sound came to their ears. At first it was like the noise of distant waves breaking on the beach. Gradually it grew louder, a rhythmic throbbing that seemed to be coming straight for them.

"Do you know, that sound could be a seaplane," said Tom, remembering the one that his father had used to find them when they had been shipwrecked on another island the year before. What an adventure that had been!

"You've just said it sounded like a lawn-mower!" said Pippa. "What are you going to come up with next, Tom, a railway engine?"

Even Tom laughed at this. He remembered what Andy had said about no aircraft ever flying near the islands. He also knew that no seaplane would be out flying on a night with no moon and no way of seeing where it could land.

But the strange noise kept on coming and kept getting louder. Soon it was louder than the sound of the engine they had first heard.

"It could be a motor-boat," said Andy. "Some of them have very powerful engines. Maybe the men are going to get away in one of those."

"But I thought you said it would be very hard to land a boat here at night," Pippa reminded him.

"Aye, it would be difficult," said Andy. "Difficult and dangerous, what with the tide and the currents. I can't figure it out at all."

The noise on the other side of the blackout curtain had risen to a dull roar. Then a new noise was added, the sound of splashing water. For a few moments they ran together and then both began to fade away.

Almost immediately there was a sudden, loud explosion.

"It's that rocket thing!" yelled Tom.

"Yes, the men have fired it again," shouted

Pippa. "I'd know that noise anywhere."

"Who are they firing at?" asked Zoe. "Has someone come to rescue us? Is that why they're firing a rocket – to catch them too?"

"Whoever it is, the two men will be more interested in them at the moment than in us," said Andy. "If one of us creeps outside quickly, they won't notice. Then we'll know for certain."

"Maybe one of the girls should go," suggested Tom. "They're good at moving quietly and they're less likely to be seen."

"Yes please," shrieked Pippa in delight, "I'd love to see what's going on. I won't make a noise, I promise. And I won't be long, honestly."

"All right," Andy replied. "The rest of us will stand in front of the fire until you get back. We can use our bodies to screen the light of the flames."

Tom and Zoe crouched beside Andy over the fire, trying to block out its light. Pippa cautiously drew the curtain back and slipped into the cold night air.

The sight that met her eyes almost made her shout to the others in astonishment!

CHAPTER SEVEN

THE BIG BIRD

Pippa took only a second or two to see all she needed. "Tom, you're right!" she said breathlessly, after bursting through the curtain back into the cave. "It's incredible, but you're absolutely right."

"Right about what?" asked Tom.

"About the noise!"

"Which noise?" asked Zoe.

"The loud one, the loud drumming one," explained Pippa. "It *is* a seaplane and it's landed right here, right in front of the island. They're bringing it in now!"

"Who's bringing it in?" asked Andy.

"All of them – the man with the beard and Fred, and whoever's on the seaplane. And the most amazing thing is that the sea is full of lights! Lots of lights and they're all under water!"

The four children looked at each other in amazement.

"An underwater runway!" said Tom. "So that's how they managed to land here at night, without anyone seeing them."

"I was right about careful planning," commented Andy.

"An underwater flare-path!" continued Tom. "Perfect for the pilot landing the plane and almost impossible for anyone else to see."

"Are you sure that no one's looking this way, Pippa?" asked Andy.

"I couldn't see anyone," Pippa said. "I think they're too busy pulling in the seaplane. There's a rope out to it from the rocks and someone on board is turning a big handle. It's hard to see, but it looks as if the rope is being wound round that."

"It sounds like a sort of winch," muttered Andy. "That would make sense. If Pippa's right, it might be safe to have a peep at what's going on. We'll have to be very quiet, mind."

Everyone agreed. They tiptoed to the opening. Andy drew the curtain back to make a narrow gap through which they slipped one at a time.

Andy came last, holding his fingers to

his lips to make sure no one uttered a word. They pressed themselves in a line against the cliff and stared wide-eyed at the scene below.

The dark night was lit up just as Pippa had described. Running out towards the horizon a line of bright lights stretched in a straight line away from the water a little way offshore. Close to them the lights were spaced some distance apart, but as they looked further away they seemed to join together in a continuous, golden thread below the surface.

Silhouetted against the nearest lights was the dark outline of a seaplane. It was

sideways on as the children looked at it. The plane was smaller than the one flown by Tom and the twins' father, but it was a seaplane, there was no mistaking that.

Beneath the body of the plane the children could make out the shape of a man. He was kneeling on one of the long floats on which the plane landed and took off from water. Just as Pippa had reported, he was turning a handle. This was attached to a drum. A rope was being wound round the drum, and as the man turned the handle the seaplane was coming closer and closer to the shore. The other end of the rope was tied somewhere on the rocks, close to where two figures could be seen watching the seaplane.

Tom gave Andy a nudge and pointed in that direction. Andy nodded in recognition. The bearded man and Fred had their eyes fixed on the seaplane. The children hadn't been spotted.

It took a few minutes for the seaplane to come alongside the rocks. There was a dull thud as the hollow float brushed against a boulder. The two figures on the island reached down and helped the man on the float come ashore. Then a door opened in the side of the seaplane and a fourth man appeared – the pilot. He was helped ashore too.

The four men stood together for a moment until one of them left the group and made his way in the direction of the engine noise the children had first heard. A moment or two later it stopped abruptly, and at the same time all the underwater lights went out!

These were replaced by the beams of two torches which zigzagged around the rocks and then swung away from the water towards the cliff. The men were coming up to the cave!

Andy bustled the other three back through the curtain, squeezing them between himself and the rock wall to keep the gap as small as possible. He was last through, and a quick look over his shoulder showed that the men were not far behind. Luckily the torches were directed at the uneven ground in front of their feet. No one was bothering to look up towards the mouth of the cave.

"I don't think they saw us, but there's no

point in giving the game away even if they did," Andy warned the others.

The four of them threw themselves down around the fire, trying to look as if they had been sitting there all the time.

When the curtain was drawn back four figures could be seen huddled round a low fire. One of them, a boy bigger than the others, was prodding the ashes absent-mindedly with a stick, beside him two girls with long plaits were talking in low whispers while the fourth figure, another boy, was lying on his back with his eyes closed.

A new voice, speaking a foreign language they didn't understand, filled the cave. The children heard the bearded man answer, but not in English. He was also speaking the same language.

"Move yourselves," he ordered, breaking off what he was saying and speaking to the children in English. "It's cold outside, let us get warm by the fire."

Tom, Zoe, Pippa and Andy got to their feet and backed away, watching the four men as they gathered round the fire. The two strangers were dressed in thick leather jackets and wore heavy leather gloves and

tall flying boots. One had a peaked cap, the other an old-fashioned leather flying helmet. They looked at the children but didn't say anything.

"Coffee?" asked Fred, who held back from the fire a little and seemed a bit shy with the two strangers.

"Yes," snapped the man with the beard. "And some light so that we can look at the map."

Fred busied himself lighting one of the oil lamps and took it over to the pile of wooden storage boxes. There he fumbled around looking for the things he needed to make the coffee.

Zoe's heart beat faster and her mouth

became dry. Would he notice that the lump of lard had been moved? Would he notice that it was smaller?

But Fred didn't appear to notice anything different. He brought a coffee pot and a packet of coffee over to the fire. Then he filled the kettle from the water barrel, and hung it above the embers to boil. In the meantime he spooned coffee into the pot and added the water when it had boiled. The smell of fresh coffee filled the cave, reminding Zoe of delicious breakfasts at home with their parents and reminding Tom of how hungry he was, in spite of the ship's biscuit and the chocolate.

When the two strangers had been given mugs of coffee, the bearded man took them over to the oil lamp and spread a map across the top of the wooden boxes. Fred stayed by the fire. He wasn't included in the muffled conversation between the three others, who were studying the map carefully.

"What was all that noise?" Andy asked him.

"None of your business," replied Fred grumpily.

"Are you leaving us here?" said Pippa.

"No, I'm not," grumbled Fred. "I'm the babysitter, aren't I? Thanks to you lot I've got to stay here for three more miserable hours until the others come back and fetch me. Just to make sure you don't get up to any mischief while they're away. I'm dog tired as it is. And now he wants me to watch over four kids – I ask you!" From the tone of his voice the children knew that the "he" in question could only be the bearded man.

"We won't be any trouble," Zoe promised.

"You'd better not be, that's all I say," answered Fred. "You'd better not be."

The sound of folding paper told them that the map-reading was over.

"My two friends and I have to leave you for a little while," said the bearded man, in an unfriendly voice. "However, Fred here has kindly agreed to stay behind to keep an eye on you. We wouldn't want you to come to any harm, would we?" he said, giving his nasty chuckle. "But just to make sure, I think we'll put that boat of yours out of harm's way." He beckoned to Andy.

"You, boy," he commanded him. "Since you're so concerned about your precious boat, come and help us. The rest of you, stay here – and don't worry. Your friend will be back soon to keep you company."

He said something in the foreign language to the two strangers from the seaplane. Then he picked up one of the torches.

"Remember what I told you," he said, looking in the direction of the group by the fire, though his eyes rested on Fred when he'd finished. Then he nodded to the two men from the plane who made for the curtain.

"Come on," the bearded man said again to Andy. "You can make yourself useful for once." He shone the torch beam in the direction of the cave entrance, indicating that Andy should walk in front of him.

"I'll see you in a while." Andy reassured the others with a smile, though he was nervous inside, and then followed the strangers through the curtain and out into the night once again.

The four of them picked their way down to the rocks where the seaplane was moored. A short distance away the *Andy* tugged gently at the lines that held her captive on the island. Andy wondered why they'd brought him outside.

"I'm afraid we shan't be able to stay for long when we return," the bearded man told Andy. "Thank you for the loan of your boat. It will save a lot of time if we don't have to bring this alongside," he pointed to the seaplane. "We can use your boat to fetch Fred and the things we need. You won't be needing it after all, will you?"

"Why do you need me now, then?" Andy asked sullenly.

"To save me wasting valuable time looking for things on board. I want the anchor and the anchor rope on deck, forward up at the bows. I'll hold the torch. You go down and get them. I'm sure you know where to look."

"Aye, I know," said Andy, jumping down into his boat and ducking into the cabin.

A few minutes later he appeared, holding the anchor and a coil of rope close to his chest.

"Good," said the bearded man. "Now go to the bows and tie the rope so there's enough to reach the bottom. Don't try anything clever. I know how deep the water is. Besides, if the anchor doesn't hold for any reason, you'll lose your boat and you wouldn't want to do that, would you?"

Andy didn't reply. In the light of the torch beam the bearded man watched him checking the knot that secured the anchor to the rope. Then he measured out a length of rope before tying it firmly to the ring in the deck. It was a good fisherman's knot. Andy made sure that it wouldn't come undone.

"That'll hold," he said, standing up. "What are you going to do now?"

"I'm going for a little row," said the bearded man. "You can go back to the cave now. I don't need you any more. Your boat will be waiting for us out there when we come back. What a pity it's so dark that you shan't be able to see where she is," he sneered. "But you understand how important it is to keep secrets?"

"I'm beginning to," replied Andy, with anger in his voice.

The two of them changed places. Andy climbed up on to the rocks and the bearded man took the torch and got into the boat. There was the sound of oars being fitted into rowlocks.

"Cast me off," the bearded man called up, "and no funny business."

The boy let go of the two lines that held his boat in place and watched as the bearded man turned her round with the oars until the bows pointed out to sea. Then he started to row and Andy's proud little boat was quickly swallowed up in the darkness.

He stood listening as the sound of the dipping oars disappeared into the night. Then they stopped. The next sound from the *Andy* was a distant splash. The anchor had been thrown in.

Somewhere out in the darkness his boat was now waiting for enemy agents to use when they came back. But Andy had no idea where she was. All he did know for certain was that it would be pointless trying to swim out to find her.

While he and the bearded man had been busy with the boat, the two strangers had climbed back on board the seaplane. One of them, Andy thought it was the one with the peaked cap, was pushing the plane away from the rocks with a long boathook. Standing on the float nearest the shore he worked the seaplane round until it was pointing out to sea. When he was satisfied that it was in the right position, he pushed the boathook through the open door and then clambered inside himself.

Almost as soon as the door had shut behind him the two propellers started turning and the seaplane's engines suddenly roared into life. A shower of spray was kicked up as the aircraft moved slowly away over the surface. If the bearded man on the *Andy* showed a light to guide them towards him, Andy didn't see it. Once the plane had disappeared from sight he could only hear the drumming of its engines out in the darkness.

The seaplane must have stopped alongside the *Andy*, to let the bearded man climb on board. It must have turned away to prepare for take-off. But on the rocks, Andy could only imagine what was going on. He heard the noise increase as the pilot revved the engines higher. The sound of splashing water indicated that the seaplane had picked up speed as it began its take-off run. When the sound of the water stopped Andy knew the plane was airborne. And as he listened the noise of the engines began to fade as "the big bird" disappeared on its mysterious flight, just as the pigeon had.

If anyone had been watching the lone boy left on the rocks, they would have noticed him bending down. In the dark it would have been difficult to see exactly what he was doing. He seemed to be tying something, his shoelaces most likely. Then he stood up, took one more look out to sea and turned towards the cliff. In the dark and with no light to help him, he had to pick his way carefully through the bracken back towards the cave.

"The men were right," Andy thought to himself. "You can't see any light at all. From the outside no one would have a clue that a secret enemy hideout was in that cave, just behind a thick black-out curtain."

CHAPTER EIGHT

YOU REALLY ARE A GENIUS, ANDY!

Fred had made himself comfortable by the time Andy got back to the cave. He had built the fire into a good blaze. His bedding-roll was spread out beside it and he was tucked up under a blanket enjoying a cup of the coffee he had made. Beside him were the oil lamp and a small travelling alarm clock.

"They've flown off," announced Andy.

"We thought they had, from the noise," Pippa replied.

"Well, don't fret yourselves," said Fred. "They'll be back soon. Then we'll be leaving you in peace," and he chuckled cruelly.

"They've taken the *Andy* out to sea," said Andy miserably.

"They haven't sunk her!" cried Zoe.

"Oh, no. At least, not yet. They've anchored her out where the seaplane lands, so they can row back here. But you can't see her. They've taken her a long way out. There's no telling where she is."

Zoe, Pippa and Tom were slightly surprised that Andy had told them all this in full hearing of Fred, who grinned when he heard that the *Andy* had been left far enough out to sea to be beyond their reach.

"Your friends don't want to hang around, do they?" Andy said to him. "They want to take off again as quickly as they can. I wonder why?"

"Stop asking daft questions," Fred grumbled. "There's nothing you can do about it. And I don't care what he says. I shan't get a wink of sleep on that plane. I'm going to get a bit of shut eye now. So pipe down the lot of you." And with that he checked his alarm clock, blew out the lamp and settled down to sleep, with his head resting on one arm. The sound of heavy breathing five minutes later told the children he was fast asleep.

Andy beckoned the others towards him, signalling to be quiet. "We'll have to whisper," he warned. "Fred's wrong," he continued eagerly but quietly. "There *is* something we can do. It won't be easy, but I've had an idea."

"Good old Andy! I knew you'd think of something!" exclaimed Tom in his normal voice.

"Shh," hissed the others.

"Sorry," Tom whispered back.

"First, let's go over what we know already," Andy suggested. The other three nodded. "Whatever these men are up to, it must be very important, because of all the careful planning and the secrecy." The others nodded again.

"They've got the suitcase full of plans and they've got the rocket in the box," Andy went on. "I reckon those are what they are going to take away with them when they come back."

"When they leave us on the island," put in Zoe, miserably.

"Now they've flown off and it looks as if they're going to fetch the person they call Mr Brown. They probably sent the pigeon to warn Mr Brown to get ready to leave. That gives us about three hours at the most to do something."

"We can't get word back to the

mainland in that time," butted in Pippa.

Andy shook his head. "If we're going to do anything, we have to do it here – on the island."

"But what can we do?" asked Pippa impatiently. "I thought you said we could do something. So what is it?"

"Hold on," answered Andy. "I'm not even sure it will work. I want you to listen and tell me what you think. It could be dangerous, for all of us."

The others listened intently as he went on. "The way I see it, that seaplane depends on the underwater lights. They're all the pilot has to show him that he's landing in the right place. You remember how the lights suddenly went out when the noise of the engine stopped? Well, I think that engine runs a generator – to make the electricity for the lights," he explained when Tom looked blank. "Farmers out in the hills use them, when they don't have any electricity cables bringing power to their farms."

"What about the noise it makes?" hissed Pippa. "Wouldn't people be suspicious?"

"Why?" asked Andy. "The only people

to come out here at night would be fishermen and from a distance that engine could be mistaken for another fishing boat."

"Doesn't it need a cable, or something to connect it to the lights?"

"Waterproof cables can run anywhere," explained Andy.

"But we'd have spotted a generator with an engine," persisted Pippa. "And we didn't see a sign of anything like that."

"Those men didn't find the suitcase when it was hidden by the seaweed," said Tom. "They could easily have camouflaged it, like we hid the suitcase, so no one would spot it."

"That's what I think," commented Andy, and the girls had to agree he might be right.

"So you want to knock out the generator?" whispered Tom.

"I thought of that, but then the plane would just fly away without landing."

"The police would catch Fred," Zoe pointed out, "and they would save the suitcase and the rocket in the box from falling into enemy hands."

"Suppose the plane took a risk and landed in daylight?" was Andy's answer. "They'd only need to do it once and then they'd be clean away with all the secrets. No, I think we want the plane to land tonight as planned. But to land in the wrong place!"

Not one of the other three said anything at this. They sat silently looking puzzled and confused.

"What do you mean by the wrong place?" asked Tom. "How can a seaplane land in the wrong place out there? There's nothing but water."

"The reef and the other island! Is that what you mean, Andy?" asked Zoe excitedly.

"Aye, clever lassie," said Andy, beaming. "If we can make the seaplane run into the rocks when it lands, it will never take off again and there's a good chance the police will be able to get out here to arrest everyone on board before they can be rescued."

"Wow!" marvelled Tom. "I wish I could think up plans like that. You really are a genius, Andy!"

"Not so quick," said Andy, waving his hand to quieten them again. "This will only work if we can move the lights and I don't know how they're held in place."

"How can we move them?" asked Tom. "We'll need a boat, won't we? And you said the *Andy* was too far away for us to get out to her."

"That's what I wanted Fred to hear," hissed Andy, grinning broadly. "But it's true in a way. It really is too dark and too dangerous to go swimming round looking for her. But, if I'm lucky, we should be able to get on board without getting wet. Trust a fisherman!" He glanced quickly at his watch before continuing.

"But if this plan's going to work, we'll have to get going now. Keep your questions till later. This is my wee surprise!"

Tom was baffled. So were his sisters. But they took Andy's word for it and listened to his instructions carefully.

Fred was a problem. He was sleeping peacefully at the moment, but if he woke up and found them all gone, he might be able to warn the men on the plane – and that could ruin everything.

Andy decided that someone should stay behind in the cave, while the others set about moving the lights. In fact he suggested that two of them should stay behind. That would look less suspicious if Fred did wake up before the two moving the lights got back.

"Zoe and Pippa, would you mind waiting here, while Tom comes with me?"

"Why does it have to be us?" pleaded Pippa.

"For one thing, so I don't have to choose between you!" replied Andy, with a smile. "It wouldn't be fair to ask one of you to come and leave the other behind. I have to go, to row the *Andy*, and catch hold of the lights. If they're heavy I'll need someone to help lift them. That makes two of us.

"Suppose Fred *does* wake up and sees that some of us have gone, he may think we're trying to escape. But if he finds you two here, he may be less suspicious. Even he must know that Tom and I wouldn't leave two girls behind on the island!"

"I don't think he likes me very much," Tom admitted to his sisters. "You two would do a better job of making him think that there's nothing's wrong."

"It's dangerous for all of us," said Andy. "But if you can stop Fred raising the alarm until we come back, the plan might – just *might* – work."

Pippa and Zoe looked disappointed. They enjoyed adventures like this and they knew they were as good as either of the boys if they got in a jam. However, they could see the point of what Andy had said. Even Tom's comment about Fred made sense. After all, it had been the girls who'd given him his tea.

So it was agreed. Tom and Andy would leave Zoe and Pippa in the cave while they tried to move the underwater lights. Though how Andy intended getting on board a boat anchored offshore in the middle of the night, *and* without getting wet, Tom had no idea!

"Be patient," Andy told the twins. "Be as quiet as you can. We don't want Fred waking up if we can help it. I reckon Tom and I have got a couple of hours. We must be back here in the cave before Fred wakes up and before the seaplane returns.

"If we can't move the lights at all, we'll

come straight back. Then we'll see if we can
make a run for home while it's still dark,
the four of us in the *Andy*. How does that
sound?"

"That sounds fine, Andy," said Zoe. "I
know you'll do your best."

"Good luck!" Pippa whispered as the two
boys disappeared through the dark curtain.
"Good luck!"

The twins sat in silence, watching the light from the flames dancing on the rough walls of the cave. Their minds were full of all that had happened since they had landed that morning.

"How do you think they're going to get on board the *Andy*?" whispered Pippa after a while. "He can't use the rocket with the rope attached, surely?"

"That wouldn't work," Zoe whispered back. "Not with the noise it makes." But this set her thinking. Suddenly she tapped Pippa on the arm. "Now I see why we heard the rocket being fired."

"When?" asked Pippa

"After we heard the seaplane landing," whispered Zoe. "That's why the rockets are here. The men use them to shoot a rope out to a plane that's just arrived, then they can haul it in very easily – just like they did with the *Andy* with that hook thing."

"Of course! How else could they get the rope out that far? And in the dark it would be too risky to fly straight in. Isn't that what Andy said?"

"I still don't see how Andy and Tom can get on board," continued Zoe.

Pippa shook her head in agreement. Andy had some jolly brainy ideas, but this was one they simply couldn't puzzle out.

No noise came from outside to give them a clue of what the boys were doing. Inside the cave there was just the ticking of the clock, the crackle of the fire and the sound of Fred snoring.

"We'd better keep the fire up," Zoe whispered, pointing in Fred's direction. "He might wake up if he starts feeling cold."

Pippa nodded and quietly the two girls lifted some more wood from the pile and laid it on the fire. The flames were soon leaping higher, keeping Fred cosy in his dreams.

CHAPTER NINE

Trust a Fisherman!

It took Andy and Tom a moment or two to get their eyes used to the dark. Even then they had to feel their way very cautiously away from the cave. The last thing they could afford to do was to twist an ankle on the uneven surface, or set a stone rolling down the slope and waken Fred.

Neither of them said a word as they crept through the bracken. Andy took the lead and at times he moved out of Tom's sight completely. Tom was still wondering how on earth Andy was going to find the boat on a pitch black night like this.

The sound of water lapping against the rocks told Tom that they were approaching the channel. He almost bumped into Andy before he saw him. Side by side, the two boys looked out across the dark sea.

"You've got me foxed," whispered Tom.

"I'll fox myself, if I can't get my

bearings," admitted Andy. "We need to find the place where they moored the *Andy*."

"It was by two big rocks, wasn't it?" said Tom. "They moored her to them at either end, didn't they?"

"Aye, they did," said the voice in the darkness next to him. "Let's try this way," and he nudged Tom to follow him. "Mind your step, we don't want to fall into the water!"

That was easier said than done, particularly for Tom, whose ankle was still sore from slipping with the suitcase when they had tried to get away in the *Andy*. He even thought about crawling along on his hands and knees – he didn't want to get left behind or to let Andy down. Andy, of course, was used to moving about a boat in rough seas, and didn't have any problem at all.

Still, there didn't seem to be any sign of the rocks they were looking for. "We should have found them by now," muttered Andy after they had been shuffling along for a few minutes. "We must have gone the wrong way. Turn round and see if we can find them in the other direction."

If they couldn't even find two big rocks close by, Tom couldn't imagine how they were going to find their boat!

This time he went first. He held one hand in front as he inched along the slippery, bumpy surface. And then his fingers brushed against something rough and cold.

"Here's one, I think," he hissed over his shoulder.

"Well done!" came the answer from behind. "What we're looking for is between these two big rocks. I just hope it's still there."

"What is it, Andy? What are we looking for?"

"A length of line, with stones piled on top. Feel with your hands, Tom."

This time Tom crouched down as he moved forward. Andy was beside him. A few seconds later Tom heard the dull rattle of a falling stone at the same time as his hand touched a piece of thick string.

"Got it!" said Andy, in triumph. "We've found the trip-line. It *is* still here! I was worried the tide might have swept it away. But the stones held it in place."

"What use is a piece of string?" asked Tom. He'd been expecting to find something much more exciting.

"You'll soon see," said Andy. "And this isn't any old piece of string. It's cod line and it's very strong. We use long pieces with masses of baited hooks. You should see how many fish we catch sometimes. This can pull in quite a weight, I can tell you! Now, I've never done this in the dark," he continued, "but it *should* work – with a bit of luck."

"Yes, but where does the line go to?"

"To the *Andy*!"

"You said she was anchored somewhere. You can't move a boat when it's anchored. That's what the anchor's for, isn't it? To stop the boat moving."

"Aye, it is. The trick is that the line is tied to the bottom of the anchor itself! As long as it isn't jammed by a rock, we should be able to pull it out of the sand and drag it back to the shore, towing the *Andy* behind it! Come on, let's give it a try."

Both boys took hold of the line and pulled gently.

"Not too hard. I want to get the feel of

the anchor," Andy warned.

The thin line bit into their hands as it tightened. For a moment it was taut. Then it shuddered and went slack.

"It's moved," whispered Andy with relief. "The anchor isn't stuck. We're in luck tonight."

They pulled more firmly now and from the other end of the line they could feel the anchor bumping along the bottom as they drew it towards them. Steadily the line came in as the boys pulled hand over hand, until they were rewarded by the sound of metal banging on the rocks below them.

Andy let go of the line and clambered down to the water's edge. Feeling around, he found one of the curved arms with a broad point on the end that formed the bottom of the anchor. Andy grabbed it and lifted the anchor clear of the water.

"Here, take this," he said, handing it up to Tom. The thick anchor rope was tied to the ring at the top of the anchor, just as Andy had fixed it. Now he pulled on this and felt the satisfying weight of his boat at the other end. After a few more tugs, the bows of the *Andy* appeared out of the darkness and ran smoothly towards his waiting hands.

"That's the easy bit," said Andy, though Tom could hear a tone of satisfaction in his voice. "You hold the boat while I untie the line. We don't need that any more."

"When did you do it, Andy?" asked Tom. "How did you tie on the line without being seen?"

"In the dark, when the bearded man got me to help with her. I thought this line might be useful for something after they caught us this afternoon. So I shoved it under my jersey while I was putting it on in the cabin. I was worried they'd see it, but the cave is dark enough for them not to have noticed.

"Then the man with the beard told me to fetch the anchor so he could leave the *Andy* out on the water until they flew back. It was down in the cabin, out of sight. So I tied the line to it down there and carried it on deck with the anchor rope. He can't have seen a thing."

"What about when he rowed away?"

"I let out enough line over the side and into the water so that he wouldn't notice it when he started rowing. Once he couldn't see me any more in the darkness I kept on letting out the line until I heard the splash of the anchor. It was a good thing he didn't row too far away or I might have run out of line! But when I heard the splash I knew that he'd dropped the anchor into the water without noticing the line tied to the bottom."

"How did you think of that? How did you know what to do?"

"Anyone with a boat round these parts knows how to use a trip-line," said Andy modestly. "It saves you having to keep moving your boat with the tide, if you want to spend some time on the beach. That's why it took me so long bringing the boat round to you to this afternoon. She was nearly stranded on the sand by the tide."

"Well, I think it's jolly clever of you!" said Tom admiringly. "I can't wait to see the faces of those men when they discover how cunning you've been."

"Let's hope we never do see them," Andy answered. "Come on, Tom, we've got work to do. It's time to go fishing!"

"Fishing?"

"Aye – fishing for those landing lights under the water."

The anchor was stowed on deck. The anchor rope was coiled neatly beside it. Andy found the oars, gave one to Tom and took the other himself, so that they could push the boat away from the rocks. Once they were in clear water, the boys sat side by side, fitted the oars into the rowlocks and started rowing out into the darkness.

"How far are we going?" asked Tom.

"I'm not sure," replied Andy. "But I've an idea that those lights may have something to do with the marker flags we noticed."

"The ones showing where the lobster pots are?"

"Aye. From what I can remember, they're in about the same area. Let's see if I'm right."

They carried on rowing for a few more minutes and then stopped. The *Andy* drifted on in the darkness.

"There must be an underwater cable running out to the lights from the generator on the island," Andy explained. "If we can find that, we can find our way to the lights."

"How do we find the cable?"

"With the anchor. We'll drag it along the bottom as we row the *Andy*. If we go across the line the cable takes from the shore to the lights, we're bound to hook it."

"Now I see what you meant by 'fishing'!" Tom was beginning to enjoy himself hugely.

"I'll take the oars," Andy suggested. "You take the anchor to the stern. Tie the rope there and let the anchor into the water. Do it very quietly, Tom. You know how sound carries over water."

Tom followed Andy's instructions and soon the boat was under way again. Now all they had to do was wait for the rope to tighten when the anchor hooked something. And soon Tom felt the rope pull against his hands.

"I've got it!" he hissed excitedly.

"Pull it up then," Andy told him.

Tom hauled in the wet rope, dragging something heavy behind it. His shorts and shirtsleeves were soon sopping wet, but he scarcely noticed as the mysterious object came closer and closer.

But the anchor didn't bring him a

waterproof cable from the seabed. When the anchor finally reached him there was only a large mass of soggy seaweed attached to it!

"Never mind," encouraged Andy. "Have another go."

Tom let the anchor slip silently into the water and Andy started pulling on the oars once more.

It snagged again. This time when Tom heaved on the rope, it tightened and tightened until he had to let go. Fortunately, he'd tied a good knot to the stern of the boat and the *Andy* slowed to a halt.

"We must have caught a rock," said Andy, leaving the oars and coming to help Tom pull in the rope. The boat slid backwards over the surface as they drew it in. When she was above the place where the anchor was caught, the boys gave a few sharp tugs and it came free.

"I'll move on a wee bit," Andy told Tom, going back to the oars and taking a couple of strokes. "Right! Try again. We should be clear of that rock now. Third time lucky, eh?"

Third time lucky they were!

Tom knew it as soon as he felt a tug on the rope. It was like catching a huge fish, but without the wriggling on the line. This time the rope became more difficult to pull in as the anchor drew closer to the surface. Andy had to come and help.

"There it is," said Tom as it broke the surface alongside them. Lying across one of its arms was a smooth wire as thick as a finger and covered with strong rubber.

"Let's see what this brings us," said Andy, starting to haul the cable through his hands.

Tom helped, and together they pulled the cable past them, drawing the *Andy* further out to sea.

They must have worked their way along the cable for a good five minutes before something knocked against the *Andy's* hull. A piece of damp cloth brushed against Tom's arm, making him jump in the air with surprise.

"What's that?" he gasped.

"It's only a marker flag," Andy reassured him. "Lift it in, Tom, there should be a rope tied to the bottom."

The marker flag was attached to a thin cane stuck into a buoy about the size of a football. Tom lifted this into the *Andy* and a length of rope followed. The fisher boy was right again!

"You pull the rope," said Andy. "I'll pull the cable. Let's see what we find."

Together they heaved away until something the size of a round cake tin broke the surface.

"What is it? A light?" asked Tom.

"I think it is," replied Andy. "Give me a hand to get it on board. The cable runs through it and out the other side. But I think it must be anchored as well."

Tom took the cable. Andy reached over and lifted the round object with both hands. The top was a piece of thick flat glass. Inside there seemed to be a circular shiny lining. A stout rim of cork ran all round the outside. The cable went inside the light through one waterproof hole and came out of the other side through another. The rope Tom had been pulling ran down into the water from the bottom.

"Let's see what's at the end of this," said Andy, laying the light on the boards at their

feet and helping Tom haul in the rope. Something heavy was coming up from the seabed.

"That's why it's such a weight," puffed Tom when there was a thud against the side of *Andy* and he could see what was coming. The end of the rope was tied to a ring set in the middle of square lump of concrete.

"Get this on board too," grunted Andy. "Mind the light. We mustn't break that."

It took all their strength to lift the concrete block into the boat and Tom pinched his finger under it when they lowered it to the floor.

"Ouch!" he cried.

"You're in the wars today. Put it in the water, that should help," suggested Andy.

"What's next?" asked Tom, when the throbbing in his finger eased.

"Find the other lights. I think they're floating in a line under the surface." Andy was starting to sound confident now – maybe his brave plan was going to work after all. "This must be the end nearest the island. That's why it's anchored by this big weight. If we haul in the cable, we can pick up the lights one by one. I expect there's another heavy block like this at the other end."

"And when that's on board we'll have the whole line of lights," cut in Tom. "Then we can row back and drop them off in a different place . . ."

"So that they stop close to the rocks!" continued Andy.

"And the seaplane will follow the lights and sail right into them when it lands. Brilliant, Andy! Brilliant!"

"We're not finished yet," warned Andy. "Time's running out. We'll have to get a move on. The first thing to do is to find out where we're going. We won't have the line of lights to guide us back here when they're all on board. And we could easily lose our way in the dark. We'll need to use the compass. You stand here and pull the cable tight, Tom. I'll look at the compass and see which way the line of lights is heading."

So Tom pulled the cable tight while Andy lined up his outstretched arm with the marks on the boat's compass that glowed with a faint green light.

"That's it," he said a moment later. "Now heave away, Tom. Heave away, my hearty!"

The lights were evenly spaced along the cable. After three had been brought aboard, Tom calculated they were about twenty metres apart. Andy reckoned they probably stretched under the water for a distance of two hundred metres. So there were ten lights to find altogether. They had a lot of cable hauling to do!

Tom's arms were aching terribly when Andy said with relief, "That's nine. One more to go."

"And the concrete anchor," added Tom wearily.

That was a struggle, and no mistake. Tom knew that he wasn't pulling as hard as Andy – his arms felt like over-stretched rubber bands. But he battled on stoutly until the heavy block was laid on the bottom boards. He kept his fingers well clear this time.

"Well done, Tom!" Andy congratulated him with a pat on the shoulder. "Well done. We'll make a fisherman of you yet. You take a break now. We need you to find the way."

And he explained how he wanted Tom to watch the compass to lead them back along the original line of the lights. "Tell me to go left or right, if we move off course," said Andy. "We must put the lights back in the water along the same line. Only this time they'll be ending much closer to the rocks by the other island."

Tom was glad of his rest. He fixed his eyes on the compass while Andy rowed back along the course of the lights. He pulled evenly on the oars and Tom only needed to tell him to move back on line once or twice.

Andy had worked out how much rowing he would have to do to reach the place where they had found the first of the lights. That's where he decided they should begin putting them back into the water. From what he remembered of the line of lights when he had first seen them, this new position would lead the seaplane right on to the rocks where it would be stuck fast.

Andy helped Tom lower one of the concrete blocks over the side until it came to rest on the seabed. Tom could manage from now on. So Andy took up the oars and began rowing again while Tom kept one eye on the compass and another on the cable, lifting the lights into the water one after the other. "This is the last," he hissed after a while.

Andy stopped rowing and helped Tom heave the heavy concrete anchor on to the side of the boat.

"Don't drop it," whispered Tom, whose arms felt as if there was no strength left in them.

"Nearly there," replied Andy cheerfully. "Gently does it," and the big lump of concrete slipped beneath the surface with hardly a sound. Andy let go of its rope at the same time that Tom put the lamp into the water with the marker flag and buoy.

"Phew! I'm glad that's done," he sighed.

"Let's hope it works," said Andy. "It would be a shame to have wasted all that effort! Still, we'll know before long."

"Are we going back now?" asked Tom.

"Yes, we'll moor the *Andy* somewhere safe, and then go up to the cave. It looks as if Pippa and Zoe have done well. Keep a good look out for the rocks, Tom."

And with that Andy pulled his boat round and headed back through the darkness towards the island.

CHAPTER TEN

Better Luck a Second Time

Tom had told the twins that they would know what to do if things didn't go to plan with Fred – and he was right.

The girls sat by the fire as quiet as mice. They kept up a good blaze and, bored and worried as they were, they waited patiently as Andy had asked.

Fred started to become restless quite unexpectedly. One moment he was breathing steadily. The next he was muttering to himself in his sleep and was rolling from side to side in his bedding-roll.

"I think he's having a nightmare," Pippa said, giggling.

"I hope he doesn't wake up," Zoe whispered back. "That's the last thing we want."

All of a sudden Fred sat up and gazed blearily around, looking as startled as the twins who stared at him, speechless.

"Oh, it's you," said Fred with relief. "I thought it was . . ." and then he realized that something was wrong. "Wait a minute. Where are the other two? The two lads? Why aren't they here?"

Pippa looked at Zoe. Zoe looked at her.

"Oh, they had to go . . ." Zoe began.

"Go outside – *you* know," Pippa continued, as her mind raced to think up a convincing excuse.

"What do you mean, go outside?" asked Fred, who was still very drowsy.

"They didn't want to wake you up," explained Zoe. "It's so dark, they went together."

"So that they can find their way back," Pippa added brightly. "I'm sure they won't be long. My brother needed to go out, so Andy went with him."

"They can't have gone very far. They wouldn't want to leave us for long, would they?" said Zoe daringly.

"Well, I'm not risking my neck looking for them," grumbled Fred. "Let them fall in the sea for all I care." Then he checked the alarm clock by the light of the fire and rolled over to try and sleep some more.

"That was close," whispered Pippa after a minute or two of silence.

"Thank goodness he's so tired," answered Zoe.

"And so lazy," added Pippa. "The man with the beard would have gone after Tom and Andy, that's for sure!"

Fred continued to grunt and twitch as he settled himself, but he hadn't tried to stop the boys carrying out Andy's plan. That was the important thing.

"How much longer will they be?" asked Pippa, who was nervous now that Fred had woken up once.

"I can't see the clock," said Zoe. "But they can't be much longer. They've got to be back before the alarm goes off – otherwise we're really sunk!"

The fire continued to crackle. The clock ticked. To the twins it seemed that hours passed before they heard a slight rustle at the mouth of the cave.

Two golden heads shot round just in time to see Tom squeeze past the black-out curtain, followed by Andy.

Tom gave a thumbs-up sign and the twins beamed back, holding their fingers to their lips in case the boys disturbed Fred.

"We found the lights!" Tom whispered into their ears as soon as they were all seated together by the fire. "And we moved them! Just as Andy planned."

"Fred woke up while you were gone," hissed Pippa.

"Did he come after us?" asked Andy in alarm.

"No. He didn't even get up. We told him Tom had to go out – you know. And you went with him."

"Well done! He could have wrecked everything if he'd found us out there on the *Andy*."

"Yes – how did you get the *Andy*?" said Pippa. "I thought you'd be soaked. But you're hardly wet at all."

"Like this . . ." replied Andy, who then described everything that had happened to him and Tom. The girls sat listening attentively.

He'd got to the point where he and Tom were starting to put the lights back in the water when the silence of the cave was suddenly broken by the violent ringing of a bell. Fred's alarm clock had gone off!

Fred must have been sound asleep again because he fumbled about with his hand for quite a long time before he found the alarm button and switched the noise off.

"So you're back," he murmured, catching sight of Tom and Andy. "If you've been up to anything behind my back you'll be for the high jump," he growled.

"I don't think we will," muttered Tom under his breath, winking at Andy.

Fred lit the oil lamp, staggered to his feet, stretched and then checked the time on the clock. "Ten minutes," he said to himself. "Plenty of time. I knew it would be."

"Plenty of time for what?" asked Zoe innocently.

"To get everything ready for . . ." but Fred was more awake now and stopped what he was about to say.

Tom dug Andy in the ribs with his elbow. They wouldn't have long to wait now!

Andy had one worry, however. If Fred noticed anything wrong, he might still be able to warn the seaplane before it landed.

Suppose the lights didn't work for some

reason? They looked good and strong, but the wiring might have been damaged when they were moved.

And what if Fred discovered the *Andy* tied up alongside the island instead of lying at anchor out in the darkness? Andy had done his best to find somewhere well hidden, but he'd had to row her in the dark and without any lights. If Fred had a powerful torch, he might spot her by accident.

There was still plenty of time for things to go wrong. Andy looked at Fred anxiously.

"You kids stay here – no going out for any reason, understand? I don't want him finding you snooping about."

The children watched Fred get ready to leave the cave. He didn't take a rocket from the box, which meant that the men on the seaplane were planning to use the *Andy* to come ashore after all, so they wouldn't need a rope to tow themselves in. A big sense of relief ran through Andy when Fred picked up the oil lamp and walked towards the entrance with it. He hadn't got a torch. That was something to be pleased about.

"Shh! He might still be listening outside," Zoe warned after the curtain had fallen back behind Fred.

"I suppose we'd better stay here till the fun starts," moaned Tom.

"Don't you worry. You won't miss the excitement," said Andy. "Just wait a while longer. We should hear the seaplane any time now."

The four children stood by the curtain listening carefully.

Then a dull drone reached their ears from far away across the sea. Almost immediately the generator burst into life, drowning out the sound of the approaching plane.

The next sound they heard was someone shouting down by the rocks. It was Fred! He was yelling, "Stop! Stop!" at the top of his voice.

"He must have noticed something's wrong with the lights," said Andy urgently. "He's going to warn the seaplane not to land."

The shouts drew closer. This time Fred was yelling at the children.

"He's coming back here!" shrieked Pippa.

"He's after a warning light," said Andy. "A flare, or a rocket maybe!"

"Quick, Pippa," screamed Zoe. "Help me put out the fire. Andy and Tom, pull down that curtain and throw it over him when he gets here!"

The two girls started kicking sand on to the fire.

"The blankets!" cried Pippa. "They'll put out the flames." And they each grabbed one end of Fred's bed-roll and threw it across the fire.

The cave was plunged into darkness.

Meanwhile Tom and Andy had flung themselves at the curtain and torn it from its fastening in the roof.

Out in the water a line of lights twinkled beneath the surface. But from the mouth of the cave it was obvious that they were in a different position. Fred must have spotted this down by the water's edge. Andy hoped that the pilot coming in from high up in the air wouldn't notice – at least not until it was too late.

But a light swinging wildly up the cliff towards them showed that Fred was coming back as fast as he could.

"Get ready," Andy told Tom under his breath.

They stood either side of the cave's entrance holding the curtain out between them.

"You kids—" panted Fred as he charged into the cave.

"Now, Tom!" yelled Andy, and the two of them pulled the curtain around the man, up and over his head, completely smothering him in its folds.

Fred gave a shout of surprise and then tripped and fell, dropping the oil lamp as he crashed to the floor.

Andy grabbed the lamp, called to the others and bundled them outside.

"Follow me," he shouted over his shoulder and set off jumping and bounding through the bracken, to get away from the furious man as fast as he could.

The others were close behind. Slipping, tumbling sometimes, snatching at the bracken to save themselves and cutting their hands on its sharp stems, they rushed away into the safety of the darkness, following the swinging light in Andy's hand.

"Down here," gasped Andy, dropping into a hollow behind a tall rock. "He won't see the light here if we close up round it."

Everyone was breathless, but as the sounds of their panting died away the noise of the aircraft grew closer.

From where they were hiding the children had a good view of the water. In front of them the line of lights glowed invitingly upwards to welcome the approaching plane.

The tone of the engines dropped. Zoe, Pippa and Tom knew that sound well – the pilot was cutting his speed. He was getting ready to land.

The throbbing of the two engines got louder and louder still. Then there was a splash and a dark shape flashed along the line of lights. The seaplane was down, and was hurtling over the water above them. It was heading straight for the reef!

The flashing shape began to slow as it reached the end of the line of lights. It passed the last one and disappeared into the darkness. The noise of the engines continued to drop. Any moment now the plane would run into the rocks!

Suddenly the night was filled with a shattering roar! A huge bang echoed round the island. The sound of splintering wood and grinding metal filled the air!

After that there was silence for a few seconds and then voices could be heard in the distance, coming from the direction of the crash. A beam of light shot into the sky – someone on board had found a torch, not that it would be of any help to them. Even in the dark the children could tell that the seaplane was high and dry on the rocks they had crossed that morning. It would never fly again.

Another voice, from the cave this time, told them that Fred had fought his way out of the curtain. As the children listened they heard him stumbling through the darkness. He was heading for the reef to help the men stranded in the plane.

"They'll all be busy for a good while yet," Andy told the others. "Come on, it's time for us to get going as well."

"Which way?" asked Pippa

"Back to the cave," said Andy. "Let's see if we have better luck a second time, rescuing that suitcase full of papers!"

"And the rocket in the box!" shouted Tom gleefully.

"It's been quite a day for rockets!" said Pippa, and they all burst out laughing with relief.

CHAPTER ELEVEN

QUITE A NICE LITTLE OUTING, WASN'T IT?

Andy was careful to keep the light hidden as they crept back to the mouth of the cave. The men would know, of course, that they were still on the island. What they couldn't know was that the children had rescued the *Andy* and were getting ready to make their escape in her.

They weren't trapped on the island any longer. Soon they could be speeding freely homewards over the waves, carrying their secret cargo back where it belonged.

Inside the cave it was pitch black. There was a smell of burnt wool from the blankets that had been singed by the embers of Fred's fire.

"Let's see how heavy this is," said Andy, making his way to where the box holding the rocket lay. He and Tom took hold of one end, the twins took the other, and they lifted. "Do you think three of us could get it down to the boat?" asked Andy. "Try letting go, Tom. Let's see how it feels."

"We can carry it with you, Andy," said Pippa when Tom had let go.

"I'll bring the suitcase," Tom said.

"Can you take the light too?" Andy asked him. "None of us has got a free hand."

While Andy and the twins moved towards the entrance with the long box, Tom picked up the lamp and went over to where the suitcase had been left. A cooing noise in the dark made him stop.

"What about the pigeons?" he called after the others. "Shall I let them go?"

"Yes, please do," said Pippa. "Those beastly men won't bother about them."

"Unless they try to use them to send for help," added Zoe, remembering why the pigeons had been brought to the island.

Tom undid the latch of the cage door, held it wide open and waited for the three remaining birds to go. They seemed unsure at first. Then there was a flapping of wings, a rush of air and they were gone. The pigeons were no longer trapped either!

Shouts and raised voices from the seaplane came to the children across the water as they struggled down to the rocks carrying their awkward loads. Andy slipped and landed painfully on his back. But he was soon on his feet again and he and the twins continued on their way towards the *Andy*.

This time they found her without delay.

Andy and the girls got on board first. The suitcase was stowed safely in the cabin. The long metal box was laid on the deck up at the bows. Tom stayed on the rocks to untie the mooring line and push the boat off, before jumping aboard himself.

He joined Andy at the oars and began rowing – rowing away from the island and its nest of enemy agents.

This time they didn't worry if they made a splash. The important thing was to get home as quickly as possible. The torch beam swung out over the water and they could hear voices from the seaplane shouting in their direction. But it never found them as they rowed steadily away.

Pippa kept a look-out for rocks until Andy thought they were out of danger. Then he and the girls hoisted the sail while Tom took the tiller.

Behind them the sky was beginning to lighten on the eastern horizon. Dawn was approaching. Soon the first rays of sunlight would be shooting across the sea to light up the island. The crashed foreign seaplane and the secret agents on board could no longer take cover in the dark. If the children could sail home fast enough, the police would be able to capture them before the day was over!

When the sun rose it brought a good strong breeze that filled the *Andy's* sails. Tom forgot the aches in his arms. Pippa and Zoe forgot their scratched hands. Andy forgot his sore back. Their spirits rose with the coming of the new day. They had had their most exciting adventure yet and now they were skimming over the waves to bring it safely and securely to an end!

"The *Andy* must want to get home as much as we do!" cried Pippa as the fishing boat broke through another small wave sending a shower of spray over them all.

"She's glad to be free!" shouted Tom, patting the stout wooden planks of the hull.

"She didn't like being trapped any more than we did!" chimed in Zoe.

Andy's beaming face showed his pleasure. His boat was safe and sound. In spite of being caught by the bearded man and Fred, he had thought up a way of escaping and of stopping the enemy from stealing important secrets from his country. And, if he made good time, he could help the police catch a gang of dangerous spies.

"Does anyone want a plum?" Tom called from the cabin. "They're a bit bruised and salty, but they don't taste too bad."

"You and your appetite!" shouted back Zoe.

"There's another tin of ham here, too!" yelled Tom excitedly. "I'd forgotten how hungry I am."

"I expect you'll soon make up for lost time," said Pippa, grinning.

"See who can spot the church tower first," said Andy. "We're going at a fine pace. It should come into view soon."

Four pairs of eyes scanned the horizon and together four voices shouted, "I see it!"

Soon the village came into view and before the sun had climbed much higher in the sky the *Andy* was nosing along the little jetty. She was soon tied up. The suitcase was lifted ashore and strong hands helped carry the long metal box with its secret contents up to the policeman's house.

Andy's father was one of the first to hear of their safe return and he hurried to meet them and find out what adventures the four of them had been up to this time!

The children were sitting round the table in the policeman's kitchen when he found them. They were drinking steaming mugs of cocoa and munching thick jam sandwiches cut from freshly baked bread that was still warm.

The policeman was on the telephone, talking in a serious voice as he repeated to headquarters what the children had told him.

"They still can't believe it!" he said when he hung up the receiver. "They won't tell me what you've found. Two of the highest ranking officers are leaving by squad car straight away. They should be here within the hour. Then we'll have a better idea."

More mugs of cocoa and another huge pile of tasty sandwiches had disappeared by the time they heard a powerful car screech to a halt outside. The policeman put on his cap, and straightened his tie in the mirror. He stood to attention when his wife showed in two very important-looking men.

It proved to be quite an exciting visit! The papers in the suitcase were, as the children had thought, all stolen.

"Hush-hush plans for something I shouldn't even mention!" said one of the officers, a superintendent.

"Are they something to do with that rock . . . that thing in the box?" asked Tom.

"They are," answered the superintendent, with a smile. "But that's top secret as well. However, since you've seen it, and since you've brought it safely home, I think I can let you into part of the secret. That's a model of part of a new defence system. I can't tell you any more, but now you see why somebody wanted to steal it and why it's so important that you stopped them."

"You should feel very proud of yourselves!" congratulated the other officer.

"What about the seaplane and the men on the island?" asked Pippa.

"You were right there, too," said the superintendent. "The man with the beard and the one you call Fred are spies. We've been trying to catch them and their boss, but we've never been able to find out where they were. They didn't use radios or any other means of sending messages that we knew of. So our job was almost impossible. We never thought they were using something as simple as carrier pigeons!"

"Is their boss the man they call Mr Brown?" Zoe asked.

"Yes. He's very mysterious and very clever. He was the mastermind behind the whole plan. From what you've told us, it looks as if we've caught him in the nick of time. It seems that they were planning to fetch him from his hideout on the mainland, fly back to the island to collect the last man, Fred, with the secret plans and the model and then take off for good."

"So you've caught them already!" exclaimed Andy.

"Fast gun-boats are on their way to the island now," said the second senior officer. "But our aircraft are already flying over it to stop anyone trying to rescue the spies. From what our pilots tell us, you made quite a mess of that seaplane! Well done! Very well done!"

Andy blushed, but he blushed even more deeply when his father shook him firmly by the hand and said how very proud he was of his son. "There'll be no work for you today," he laughed. "I think you've earned a day off, don't you?"

"So do I," agreed the superintendent. "Quite a nice little outing, wasn't it?"

"Fine," said Andy. "The best picnic we've ever had! I could do with a few more like it, sir!"

"So could we!" said the others as they went to the door to wave goodbye to the two senior officers.

It was still quite early in the morning when Tom, Pippa and Zoe ran back up the path to their house. They saw smoke rising from the chimney. Jeanie was up getting breakfast.

"My, you're early birds this morning! I didn't hear a thing when you left the house," she greeted them as they tumbled through the kitchen door. "Are you ready for your porridge? And there are scrambled eggs to follow. I expect you've had a few adventures this morning already."

"Just a few, Jeanie!" said Zoe, helping to ladle hot creamy porridge into four bowls. "Just a few!"